ANN M. MARTIN

THE BABY-SITTERS CLUB

THE TRUTH ABOUT STACEY

A GRAPHIC NOVEL BY

RAINA TELGEMEIER

WITH COLOR BY BRADEN LAMB

An Imprint of
■SCHOLASTIC

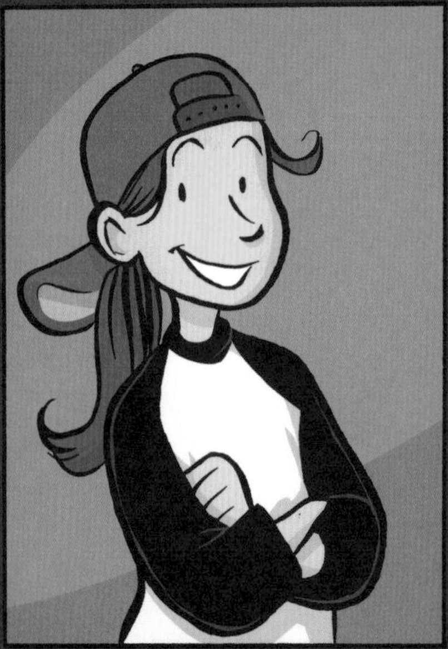

KRISTY THOMAS
PRESIDENT

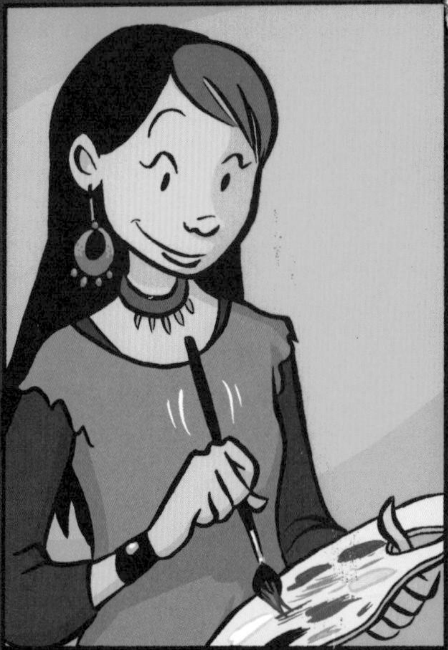

CLAUDIA KISHI
VICE PRESIDENT

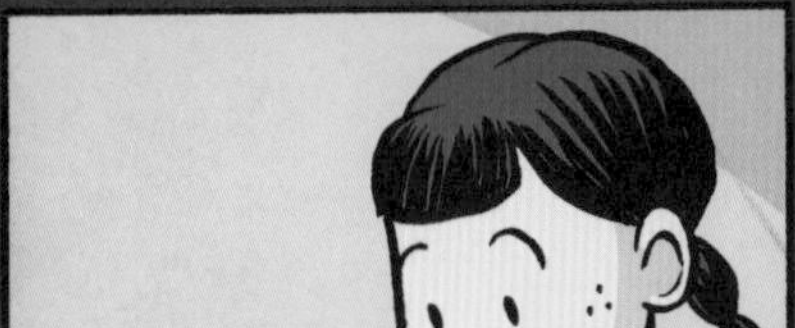
A Wrinkle in Time

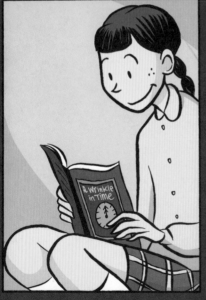

MARY ANNE SPIER
SECRETARY

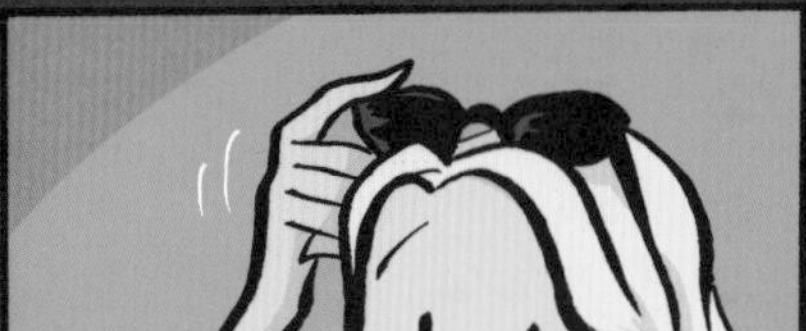

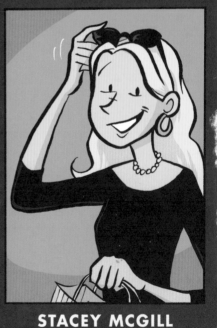

STACEY MCGILL
TREASURER

CHAPTER 1

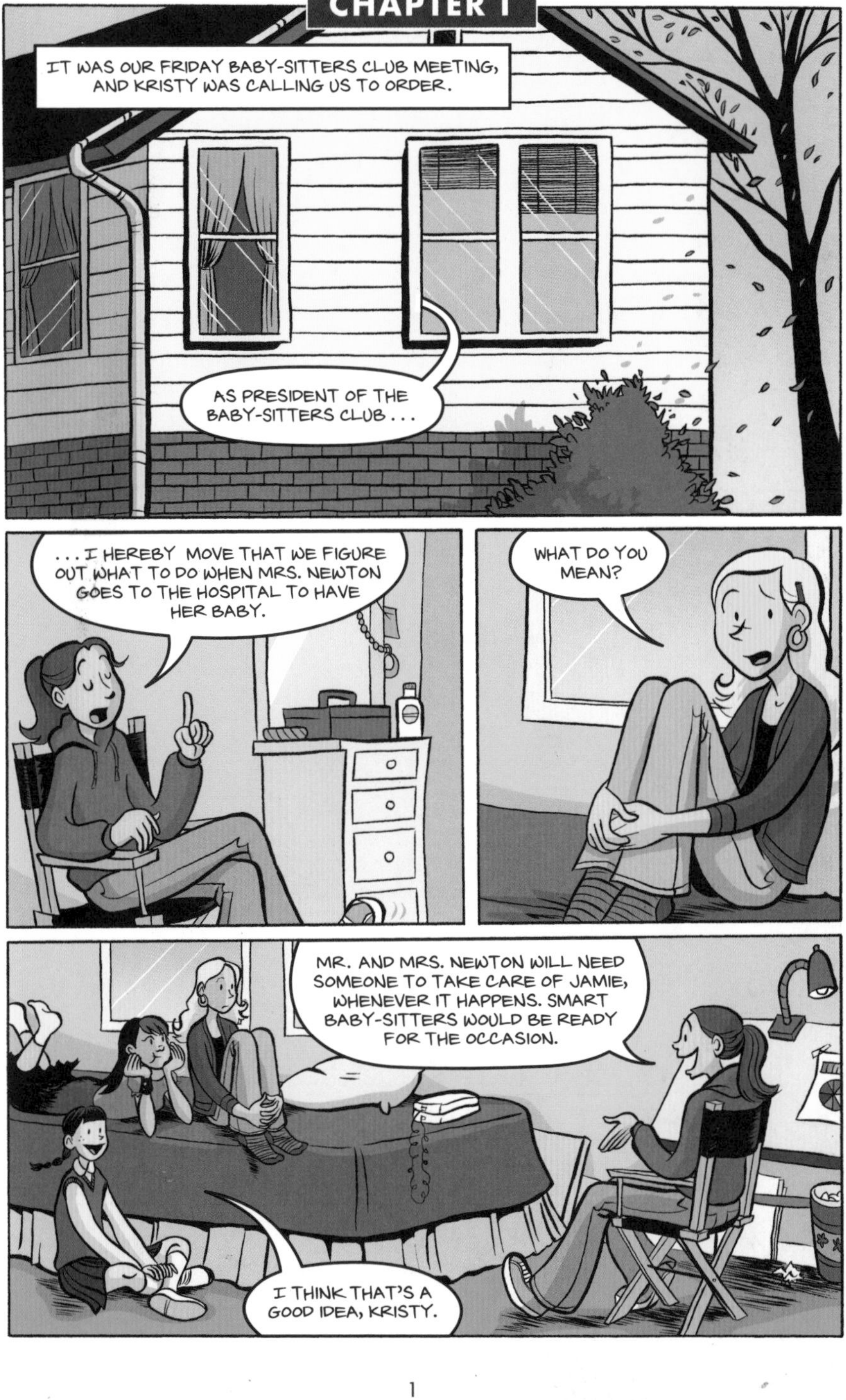
IT WAS OUR FRIDAY BABY-SITTERS CLUB MEETING, AND KRISTY WAS CALLING US TO ORDER.
AS PRESIDENT OF THE BABY-SITTERS CLUB . . .
. . . I HEREBY MOVE THAT WE FIGURE OUT WHAT TO DO WHEN MRS. NEWTON GOES TO THE HOSPITAL TO HAVE HER BABY.
WHAT DO YOU MEAN?
MR. AND MRS. NEWTON WILL NEED SOMEONE TO TAKE CARE OF JAMIE, WHENEVER IT HAPPENS. SMART BABY-SITTERS WOULD BE READY FOR THE OCCASION.
I THINK THAT'S A GOOD IDEA, KRISTY.

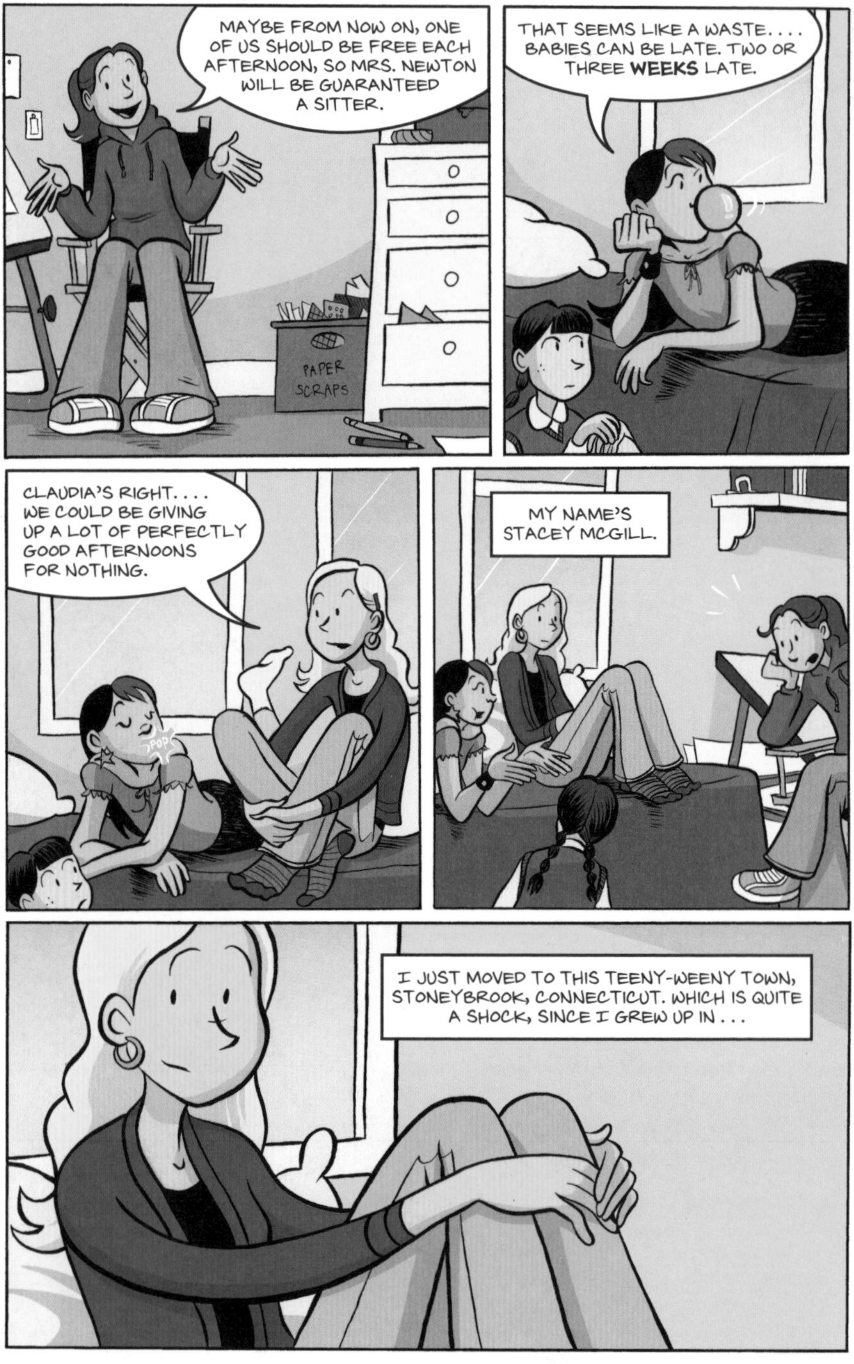
MAYBE FROM NOW ON, ONE OF US SHOULD BE FREE EACH AFTERNOON, SO MRS. NEWTON WILL BE GUARANTEED A SITTER.
PAPER SCRAPS
THAT SEEMS LIKE A WASTE. . . . BABIES CAN BE LATE. TWO OR THREE WEEKS LATE.
CLAUDIA'S RIGHT. . . . WE COULD BE GIVING UP A LOT OF PERFECTLY GOOD AFTERNOONS FOR NOTHING.
POP
MY NAME'S STACEY MCGILL.
I JUST MOVED TO THIS TEENY-WEENY TOWN, STONEYBROOK, CONNECTICUT. WHICH IS QUITE A SHOCK, SINCE I GREW UP IN . . .

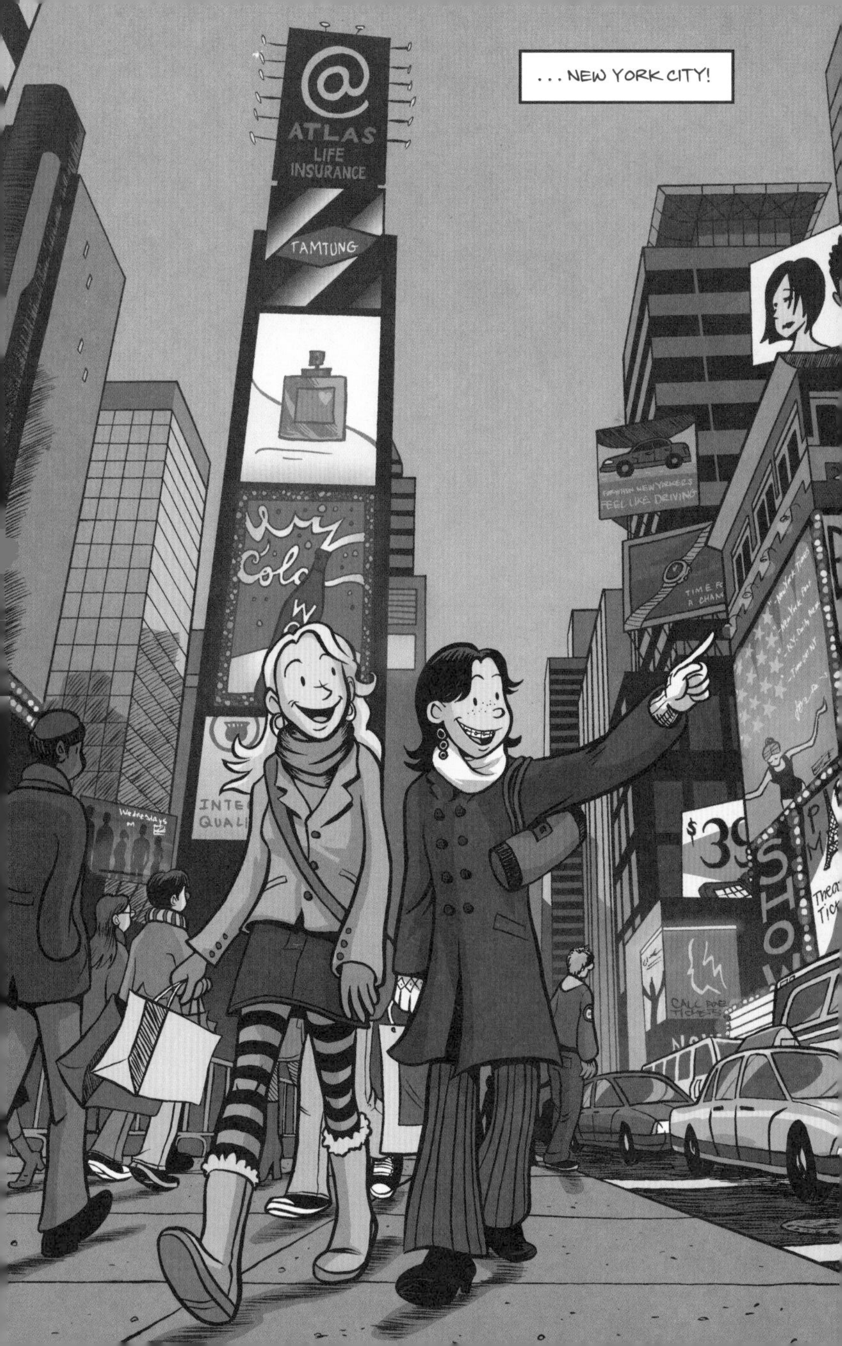
. . . NEW YORK CITY!
ATLAS
LIFE
INSURANCE
TAMTUNG
FEEL LIKE DRIVING
SHOW

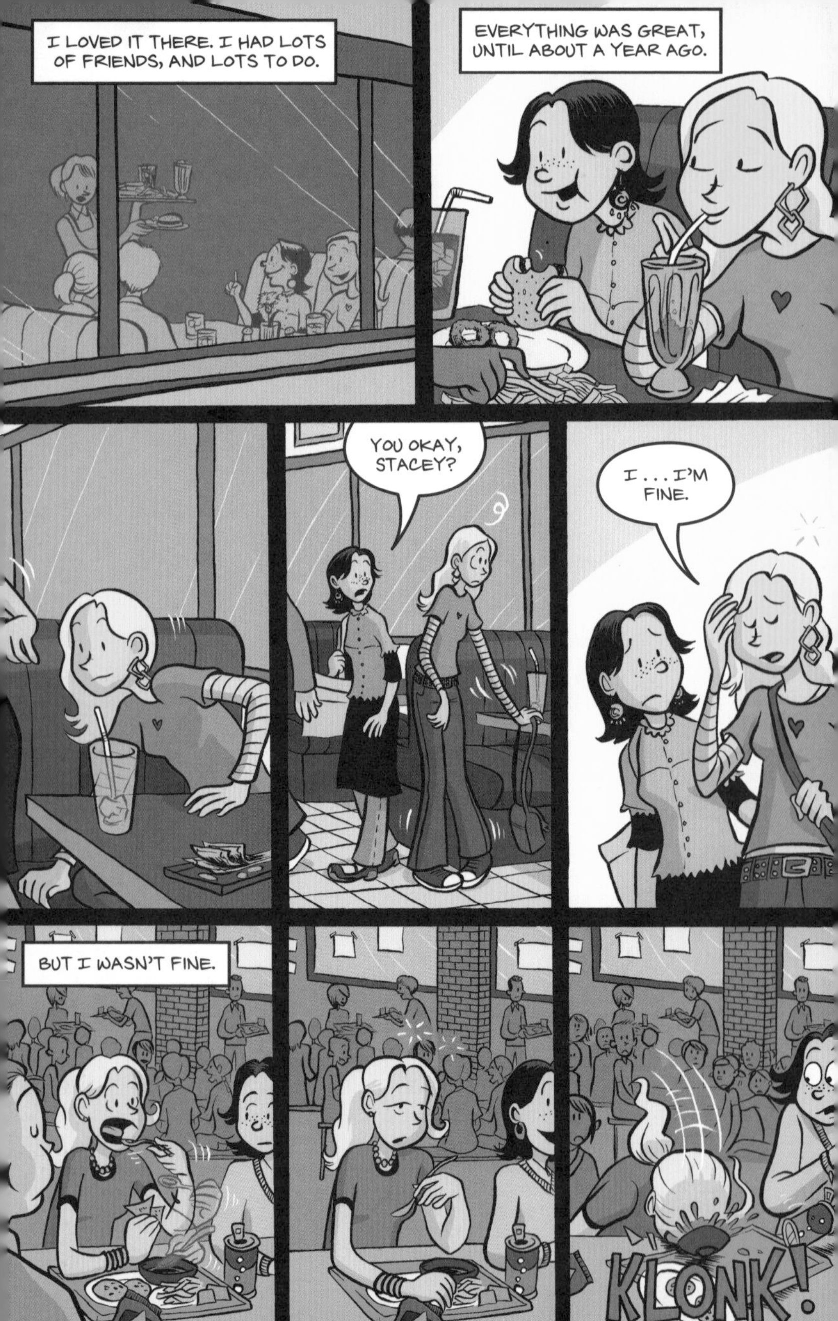
I LOVED IT THERE. I HAD LOTS OF FRIENDS, AND LOTS TO DO.
EVERYTHING WAS GREAT, UNTIL ABOUT A YEAR AGO.
YOU OKAY, STACEY?
I . . . I'M FINE.
BUT I WASN'T FINE.
KLONK!

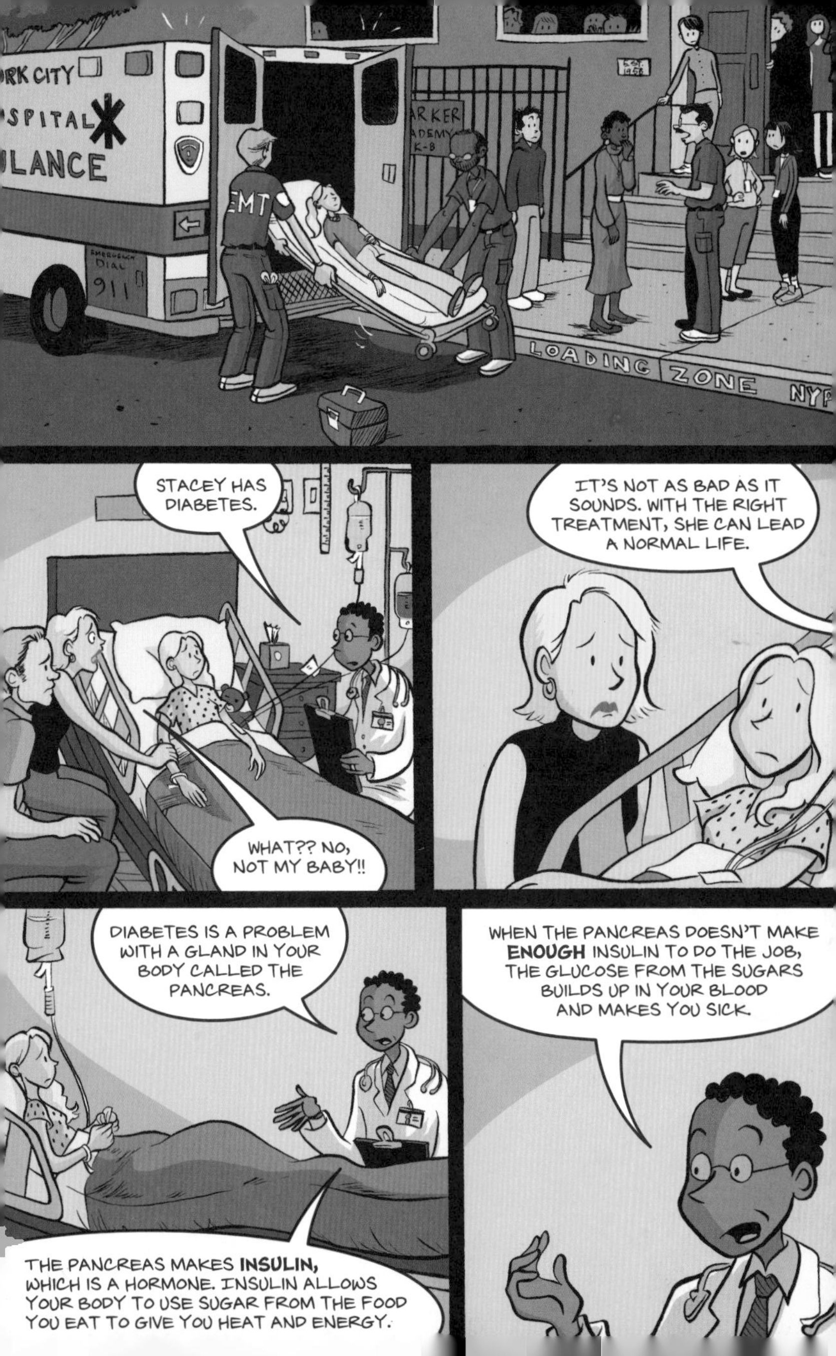

ORK CITY
SPITAL
ULANCE
EMT
EMERGENCY DIAL 911
ARKER
ADEMY
K-8
LOADING ZONE NYP
STACEY HAS DIABETES.
WHAT?? NO, NOT MY BABY!!
IT'S NOT AS BAD AS IT SOUNDS. WITH THE RIGHT TREATMENT, SHE CAN LEAD A NORMAL LIFE.
DIABETES IS A PROBLEM WITH A GLAND IN YOUR BODY CALLED THE PANCREAS.
THE PANCREAS MAKES **INSULIN,** WHICH IS A HORMONE. INSULIN ALLOWS YOUR BODY TO USE SUGAR FROM THE FOOD YOU EAT TO GIVE YOU HEAT AND ENERGY.
WHEN THE PANCREAS DOESN'T MAKE **ENOUGH** INSULIN TO DO THE JOB, THE GLUCOSE FROM THE SUGARS BUILDS UP IN YOUR BLOOD AND MAKES YOU SICK.

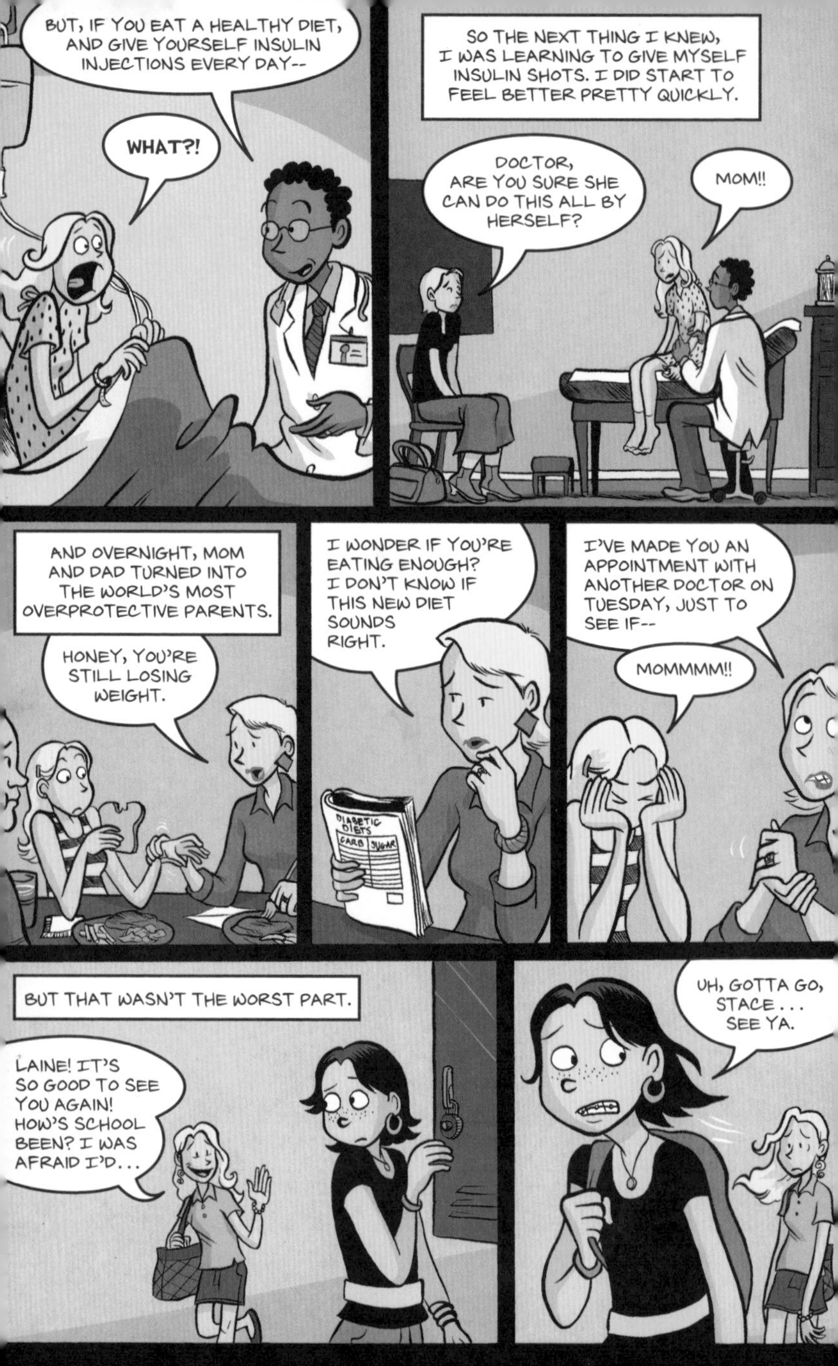
BUT, IF YOU EAT A HEALTHY DIET, AND GIVE YOURSELF INSULIN INJECTIONS EVERY DAY--
WHAT?!
SO THE NEXT THING I KNEW, I WAS LEARNING TO GIVE MYSELF INSULIN SHOTS. I DID START TO FEEL BETTER PRETTY QUICKLY.
DOCTOR, ARE YOU SURE SHE CAN DO THIS ALL BY HERSELF?
MOM!!
AND OVERNIGHT, MOM AND DAD TURNED INTO THE WORLD'S MOST OVERPROTECTIVE PARENTS.
HONEY, YOU'RE STILL LOSING WEIGHT.
I WONDER IF YOU'RE EATING ENOUGH? I DON'T KNOW IF THIS NEW DIET SOUNDS RIGHT.
DIABETIC DIETS
CARB SUGAR
I'VE MADE YOU AN APPOINTMENT WITH ANOTHER DOCTOR ON TUESDAY, JUST TO SEE IF--
MOMMMM!!
BUT THAT WASN'T THE WORST PART.
LAINE! IT'S SO GOOD TO SEE YOU AGAIN! HOW'S SCHOOL BEEN? I WAS AFRAID I'D . . .
UH, GOTTA GO, STACE . . . SEE YA.

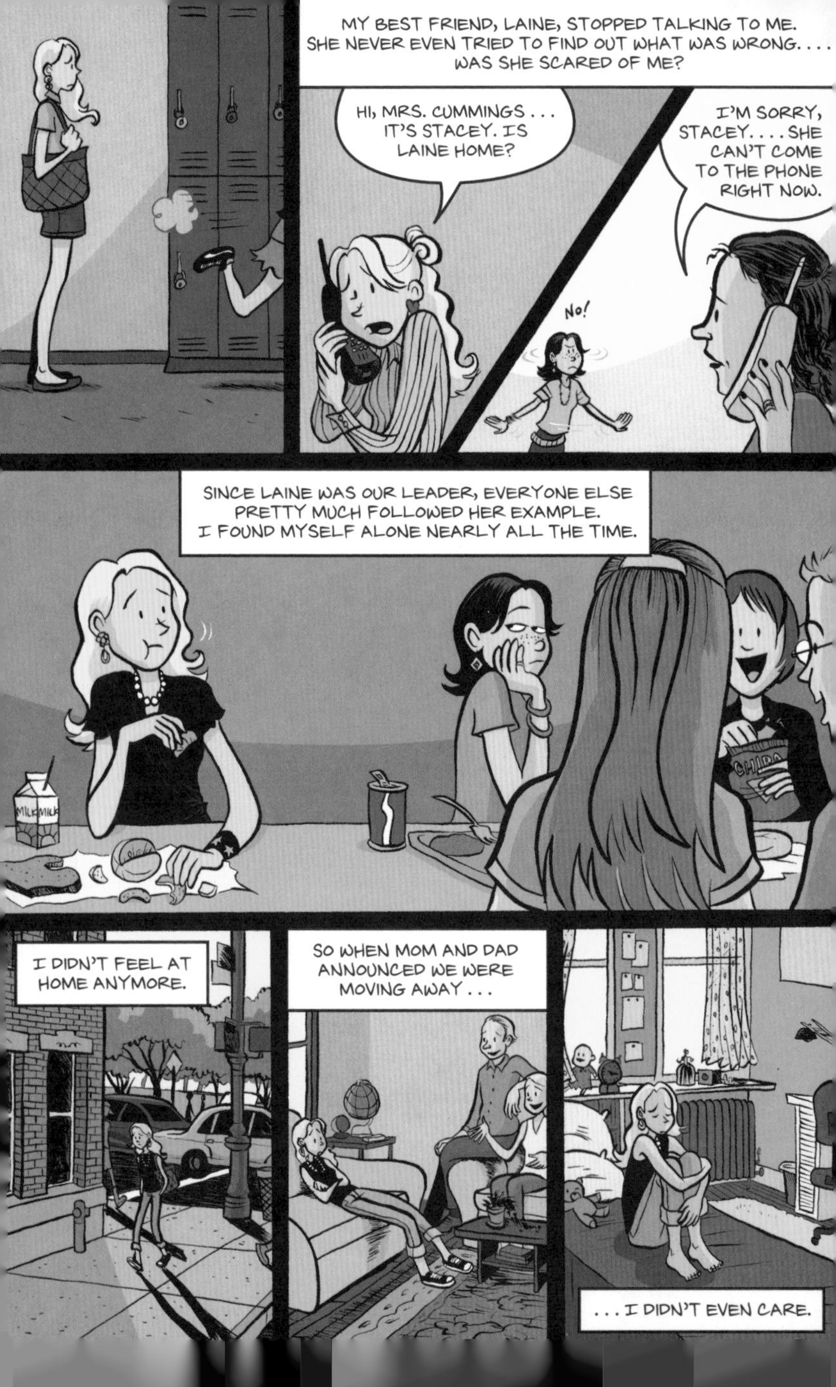
MY BEST FRIEND, LAINE, STOPPED TALKING TO ME. SHE NEVER EVEN TRIED TO FIND OUT WHAT WAS WRONG. . . . WAS SHE SCARED OF ME?
HI, MRS. CUMMINGS . . . IT'S STACEY. IS LAINE HOME?
I'M SORRY, STACEY. . . . SHE CAN'T COME TO THE PHONE RIGHT NOW.
NO!
SINCE LAINE WAS OUR LEADER, EVERYONE ELSE PRETTY MUCH FOLLOWED HER EXAMPLE. I FOUND MYSELF ALONE NEARLY ALL THE TIME.
MILK MILK
CHIPS
I DIDN'T FEEL AT HOME ANYMORE.
SO WHEN MOM AND DAD ANNOUNCED WE WERE MOVING AWAY . . .
. . . I DIDN'T EVEN CARE.

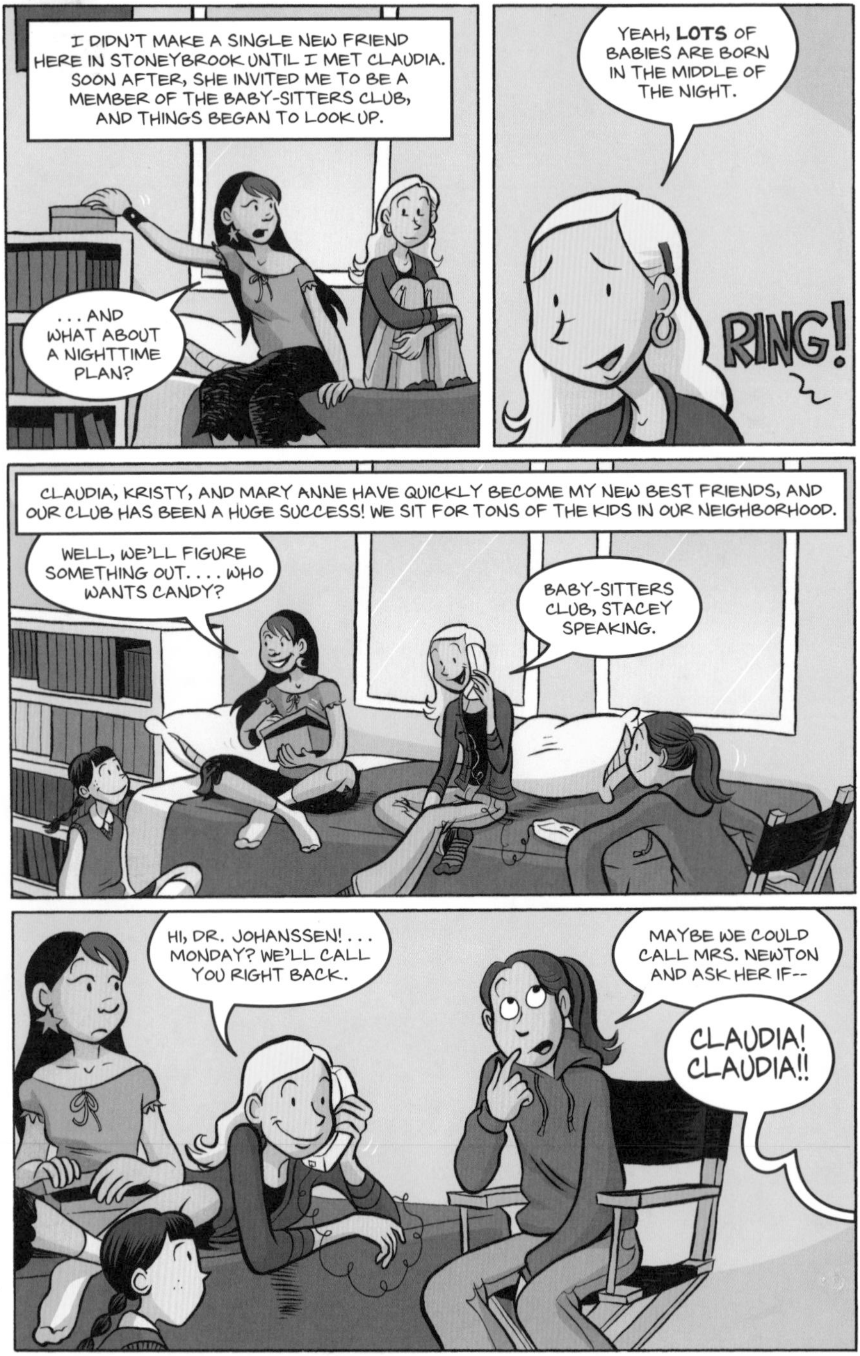
I DIDN'T MAKE A SINGLE NEW FRIEND HERE IN STONEYBROOK UNTIL I MET CLAUDIA. SOON AFTER, SHE INVITED ME TO BE A MEMBER OF THE BABY-SITTERS CLUB, AND THINGS BEGAN TO LOOK UP.
. . . AND WHAT ABOUT A NIGHTTIME PLAN?
YEAH, **LOTS** OF BABIES ARE BORN IN THE MIDDLE OF THE NIGHT.
RING!
CLAUDIA, KRISTY, AND MARY ANNE HAVE QUICKLY BECOME MY NEW BEST FRIENDS, AND OUR CLUB HAS BEEN A HUGE SUCCESS! WE SIT FOR TONS OF THE KIDS IN OUR NEIGHBORHOOD.
WELL, WE'LL FIGURE SOMETHING OUT. . . . WHO WANTS CANDY?
BABY-SITTERS CLUB, STACEY SPEAKING.
HI, DR. JOHANSSEN! . . . MONDAY? WE'LL CALL YOU RIGHT BACK.
MAYBE WE COULD CALL MRS. NEWTON AND ASK HER IF--
CLAUDIA! CLAUDIA!!

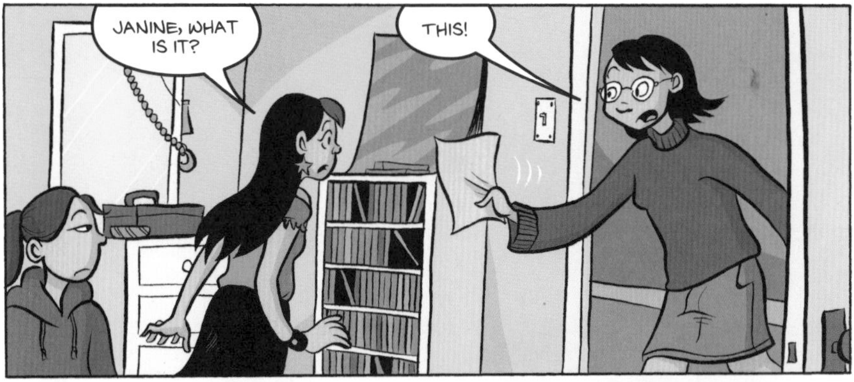
JANINE, WHAT IS IT?
THIS!

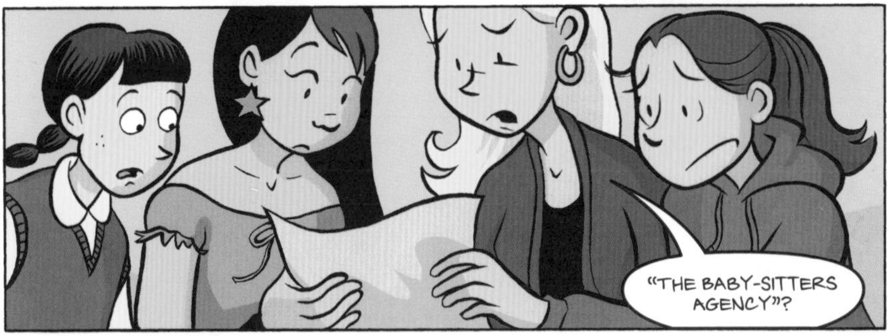
"THE BABY-SITTERS AGENCY"?

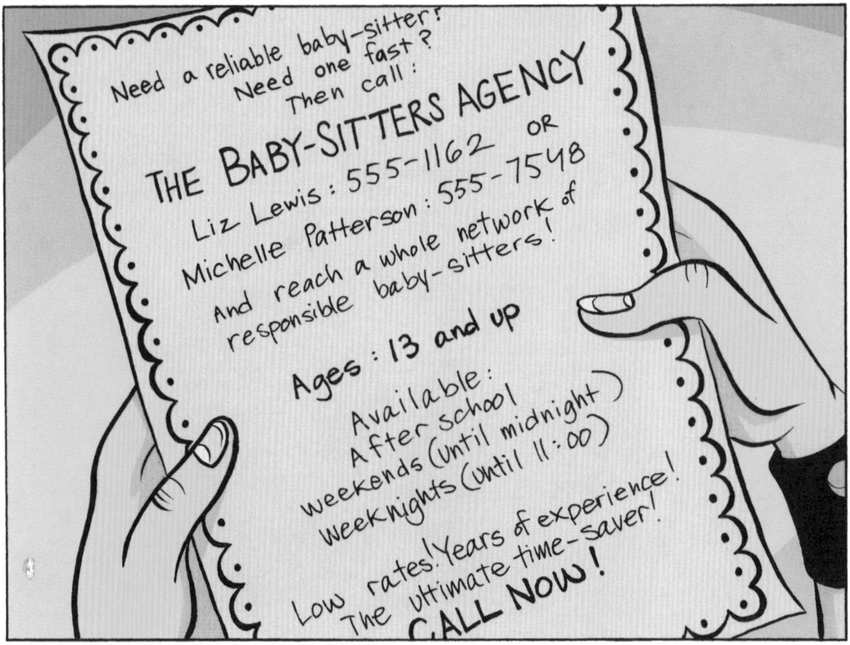
Need a reliable baby-sitter?
Need one fast?
Then call:
THE BABY-SITTERS AGENCY
Liz Lewis: 555-1162 OR
Michelle Patterson: 555-7548
And reach a whole network of responsible baby-sitters!
Ages: 13 and up
Available:
After school
weekends (until midnight)
weeknights (until 11:00)
Low rates! Years of experience!
The ultimate time-saver!
CALL NOW!

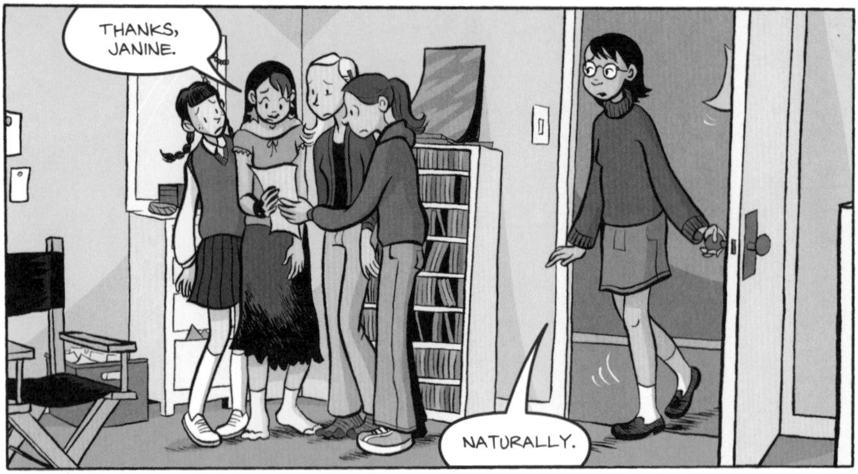
THANKS, JANINE.
NATURALLY.

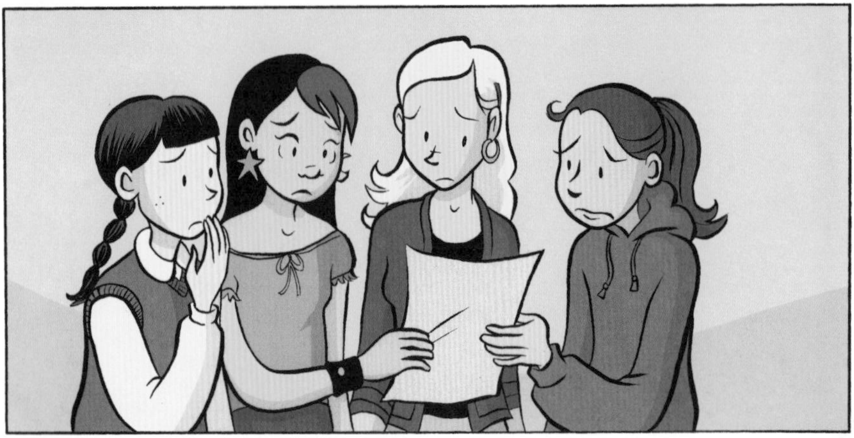

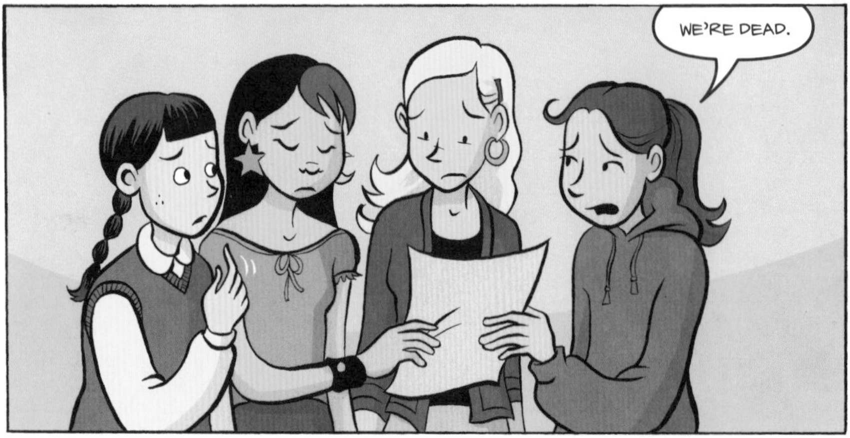
WE'RE DEAD.

CHAPTER 2

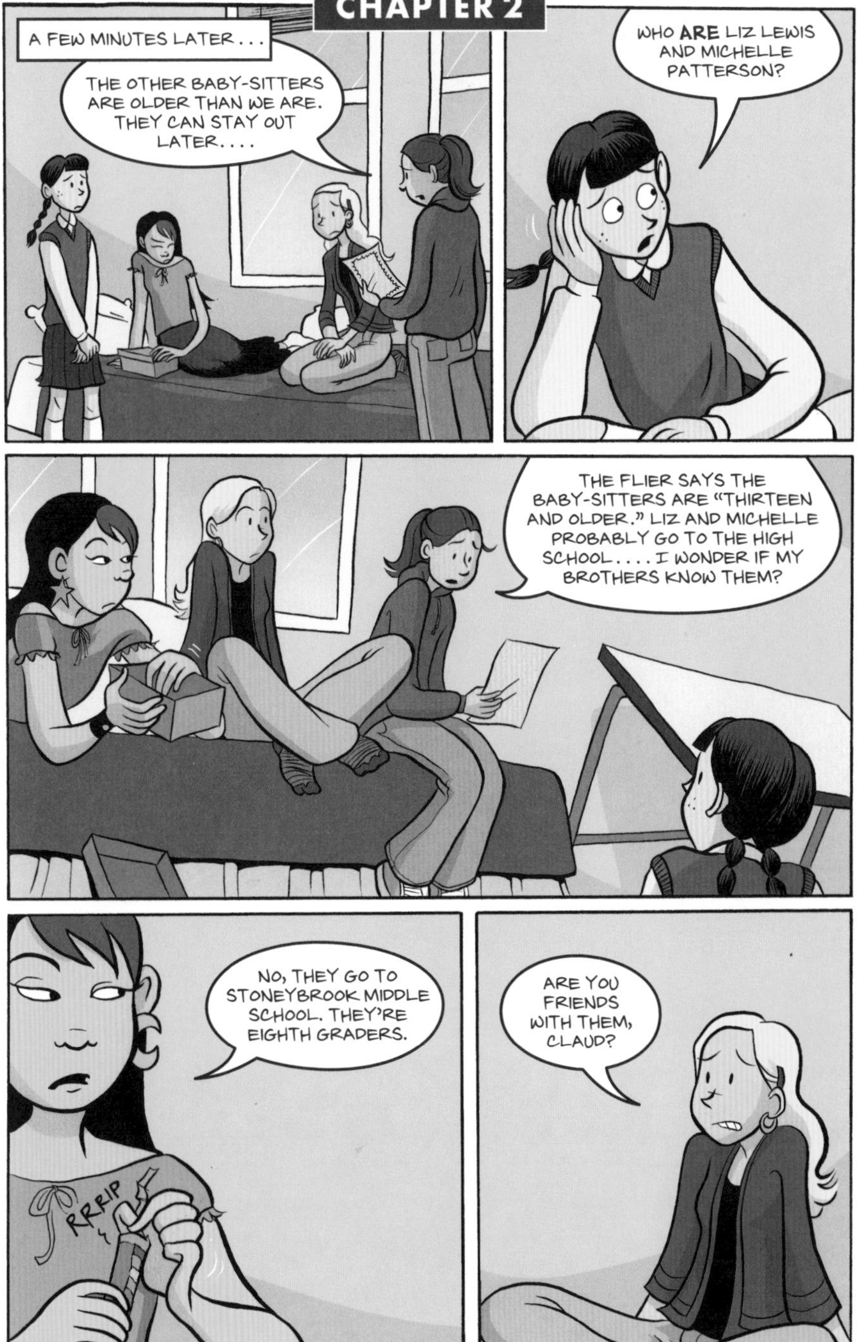
A FEW MINUTES LATER . . .
THE OTHER BABY-SITTERS ARE OLDER THAN WE ARE. THEY CAN STAY OUT LATER. . . .
WHO **ARE** LIZ LEWIS AND MICHELLE PATTERSON?
THE FLIER SAYS THE BABY-SITTERS ARE "THIRTEEN AND OLDER." LIZ AND MICHELLE PROBABLY GO TO THE HIGH SCHOOL. . . . I WONDER IF MY BROTHERS KNOW THEM?
NO, THEY GO TO STONEYBROOK MIDDLE SCHOOL. THEY'RE EIGHTH GRADERS.
RRRIP
ARE YOU FRIENDS WITH THEM, CLAUD?

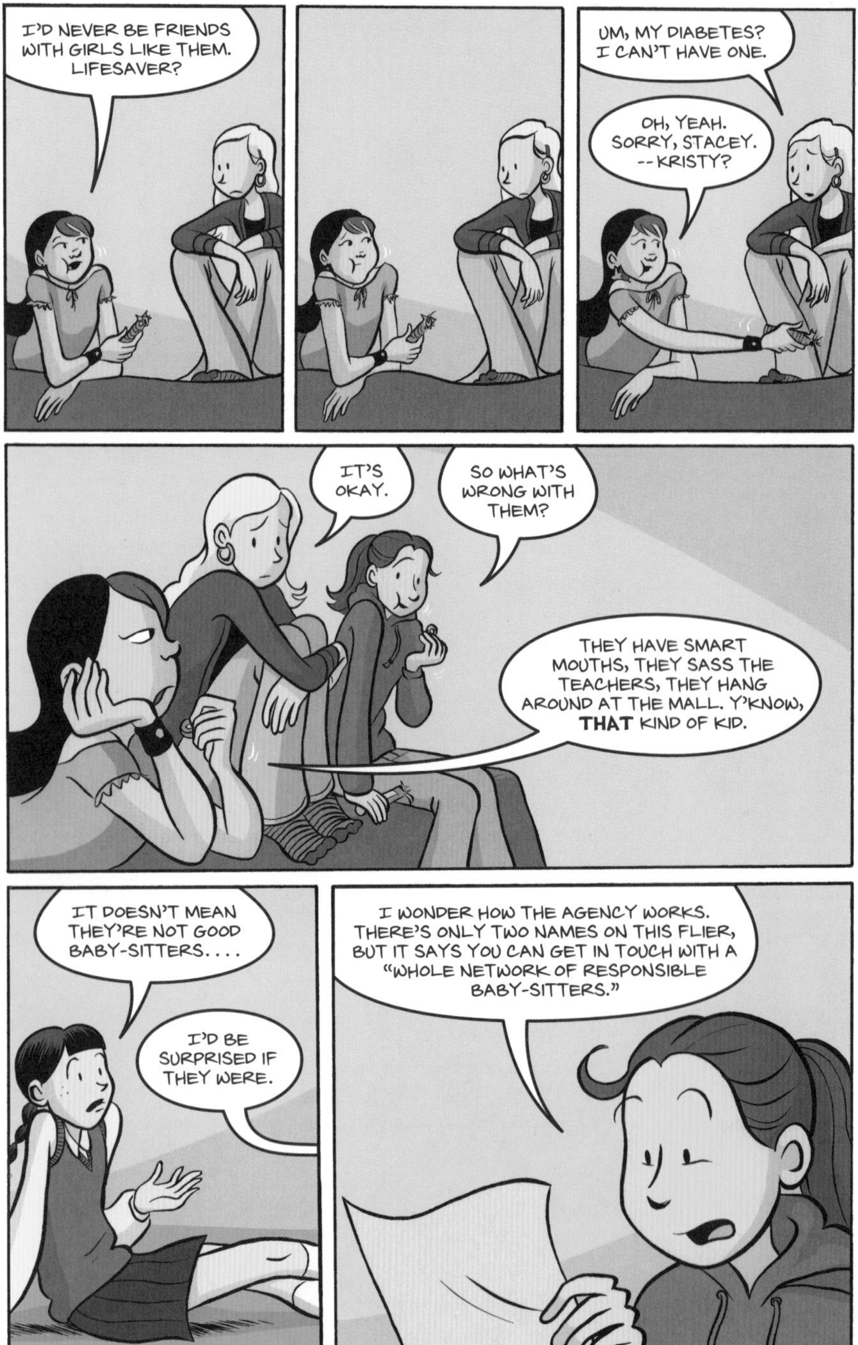
I'D NEVER BE FRIENDS WITH GIRLS LIKE THEM. LIFESAVER?
UM, MY DIABETES? I CAN'T HAVE ONE.
OH, YEAH. SORRY, STACEY. --KRISTY?
IT'S OKAY.
SO WHAT'S WRONG WITH THEM?
THEY HAVE SMART MOUTHS, THEY SASS THE TEACHERS, THEY HANG AROUND AT THE MALL. Y'KNOW, **THAT** KIND OF KID.
IT DOESN'T MEAN THEY'RE NOT GOOD BABY-SITTERS. . . .
I'D BE SURPRISED IF THEY WERE.
I WONDER HOW THE AGENCY WORKS. THERE'S ONLY TWO NAMES ON THIS FLIER, BUT IT SAYS YOU CAN GET IN TOUCH WITH A "WHOLE NETWORK OF RESPONSIBLE BABY-SITTERS."

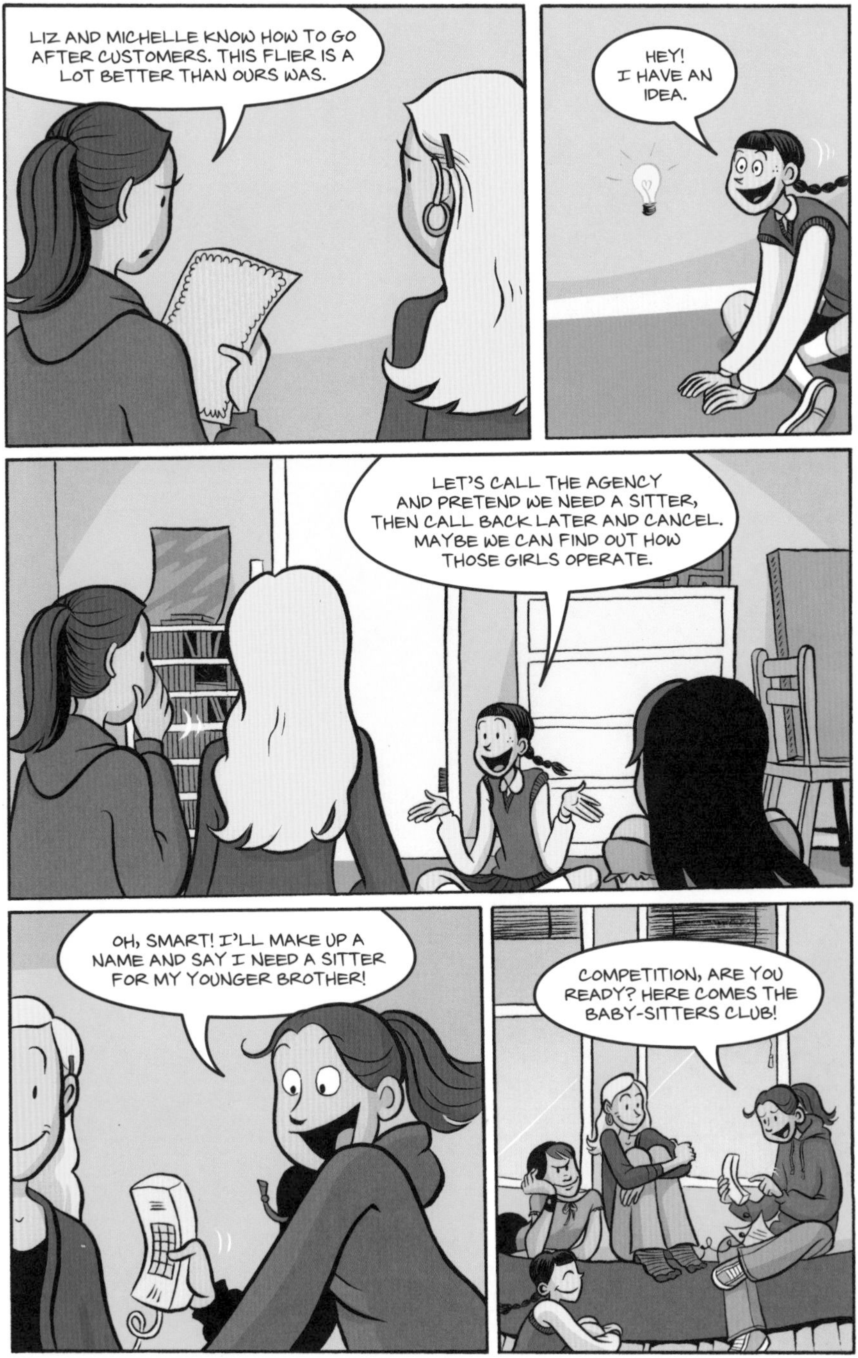
LIZ AND MICHELLE KNOW HOW TO GO AFTER CUSTOMERS. THIS FLIER IS A LOT BETTER THAN OURS WAS.
HEY! I HAVE AN IDEA.
LET'S CALL THE AGENCY AND PRETEND WE NEED A SITTER, THEN CALL BACK LATER AND CANCEL. MAYBE WE CAN FIND OUT HOW THOSE GIRLS OPERATE.
OH, SMART! I'LL MAKE UP A NAME AND SAY I NEED A SITTER FOR MY YOUNGER BROTHER!
COMPETITION, ARE YOU READY? HERE COMES THE BABY-SITTERS CLUB!

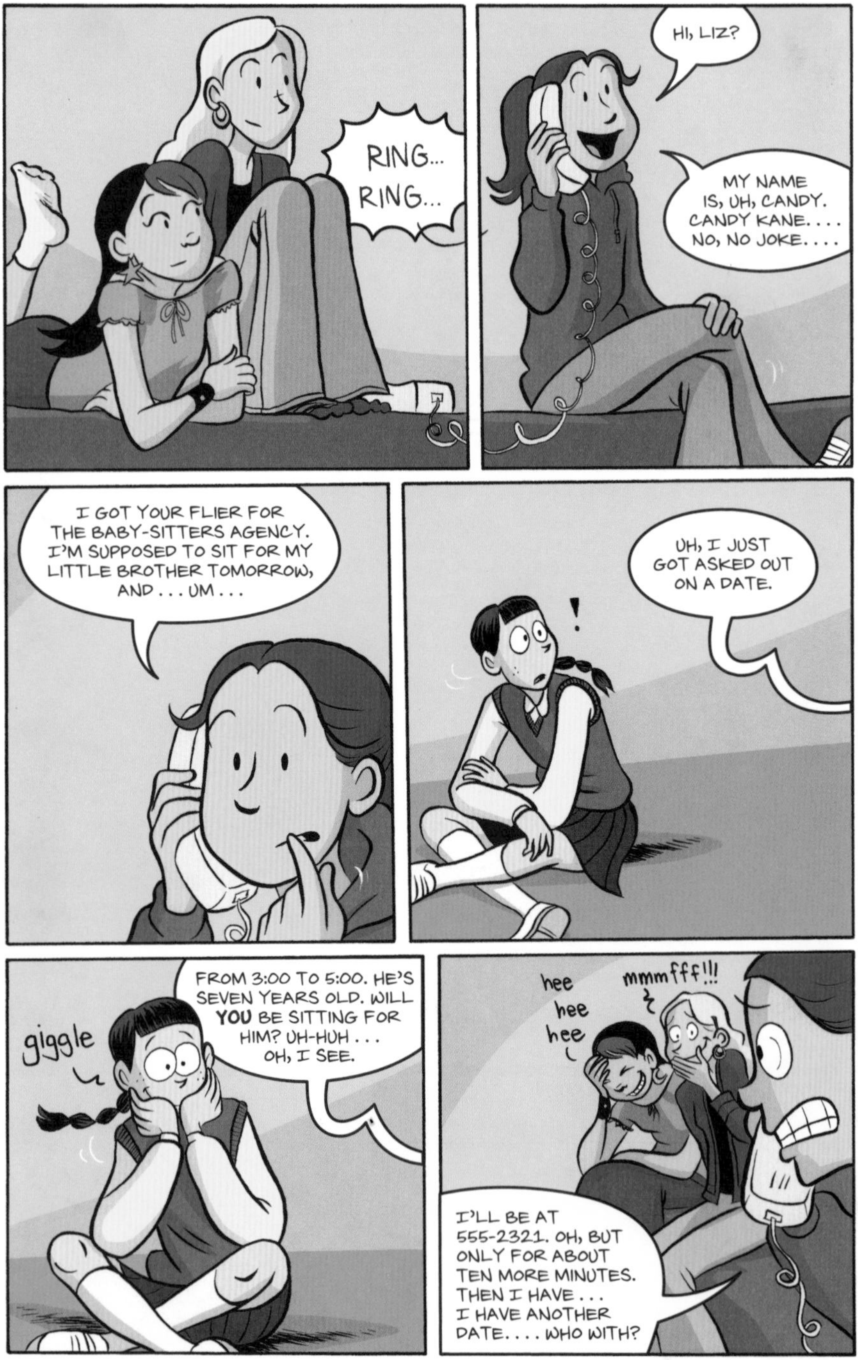
RING...
RING...
HI, LIZ?
MY NAME IS, UH, CANDY. CANDY KANE. . . . NO, NO JOKE. . . .
I GOT YOUR FLIER FOR THE BABY-SITTERS AGENCY. I'M SUPPOSED TO SIT FOR MY LITTLE BROTHER TOMORROW, AND . . . UM . . .
UH, I JUST GOT ASKED OUT ON A DATE.
!
FROM 3:00 TO 5:00. HE'S SEVEN YEARS OLD. WILL **YOU** BE SITTING FOR HIM? UH-HUH . . . OH, I SEE.
giggle
hee hee hee
mmmfff!!!
I'LL BE AT 555-2321. OH, BUT ONLY FOR ABOUT TEN MORE MINUTES. THEN I HAVE . . . I HAVE ANOTHER DATE. . . . WHO WITH?

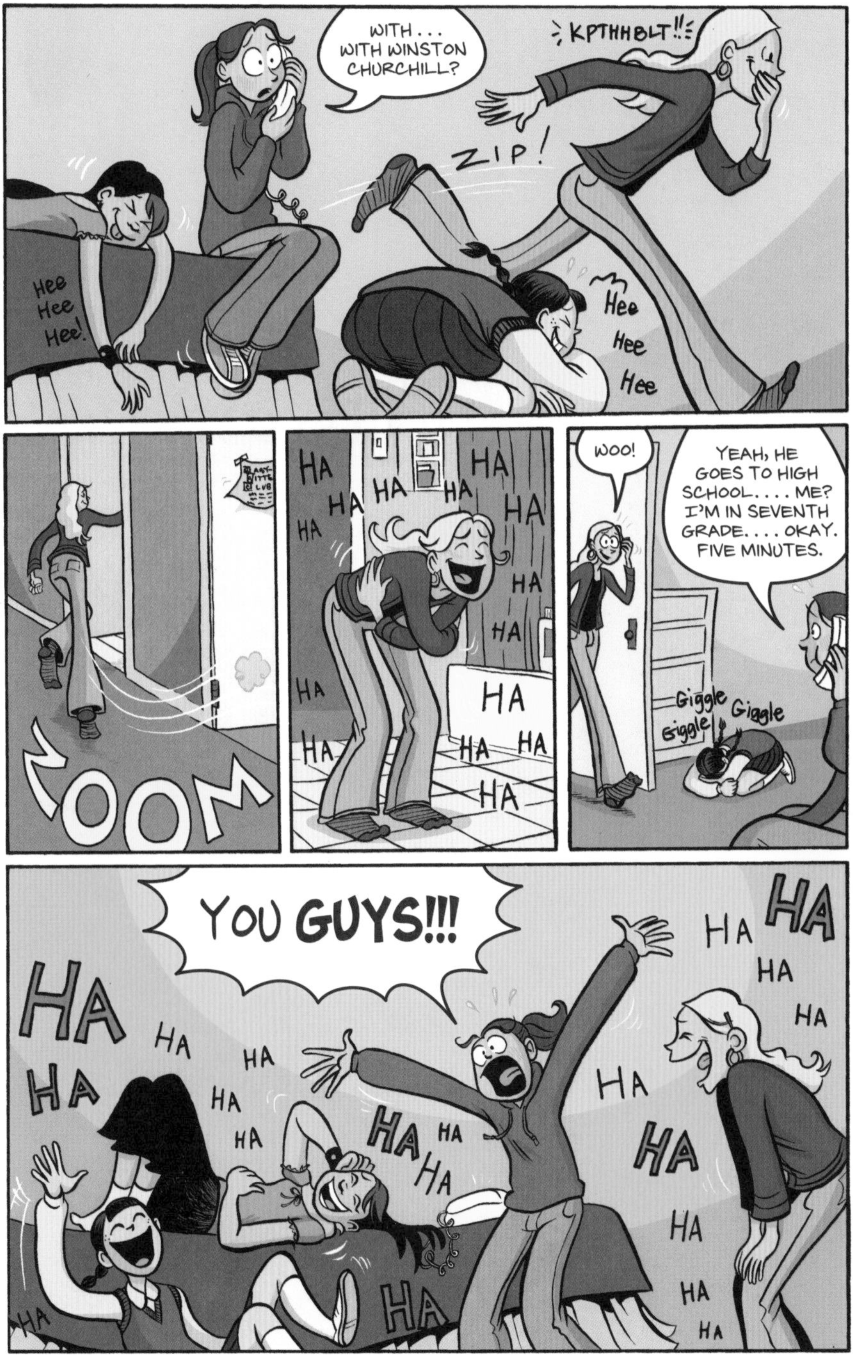
WITH . . .
WITH WINSTON CHURCHILL?
KPTHHBLT!!
ZIP!
Hee Hee Hee!
Hee Hee Hee
ZOOM
HA HA HA HA HA HA HA HA HA HA HA HA HA HA HA HA HA
WOO!
YEAH, HE GOES TO HIGH SCHOOL. . . . ME? I'M IN SEVENTH GRADE. . . . OKAY. FIVE MINUTES.
Giggle Giggle Giggle
YOU GUYS!!!
HA HA HA HA HA HA HA HA HA HA HA HA HA HA HA HA HA HA HA HA HA HA HA

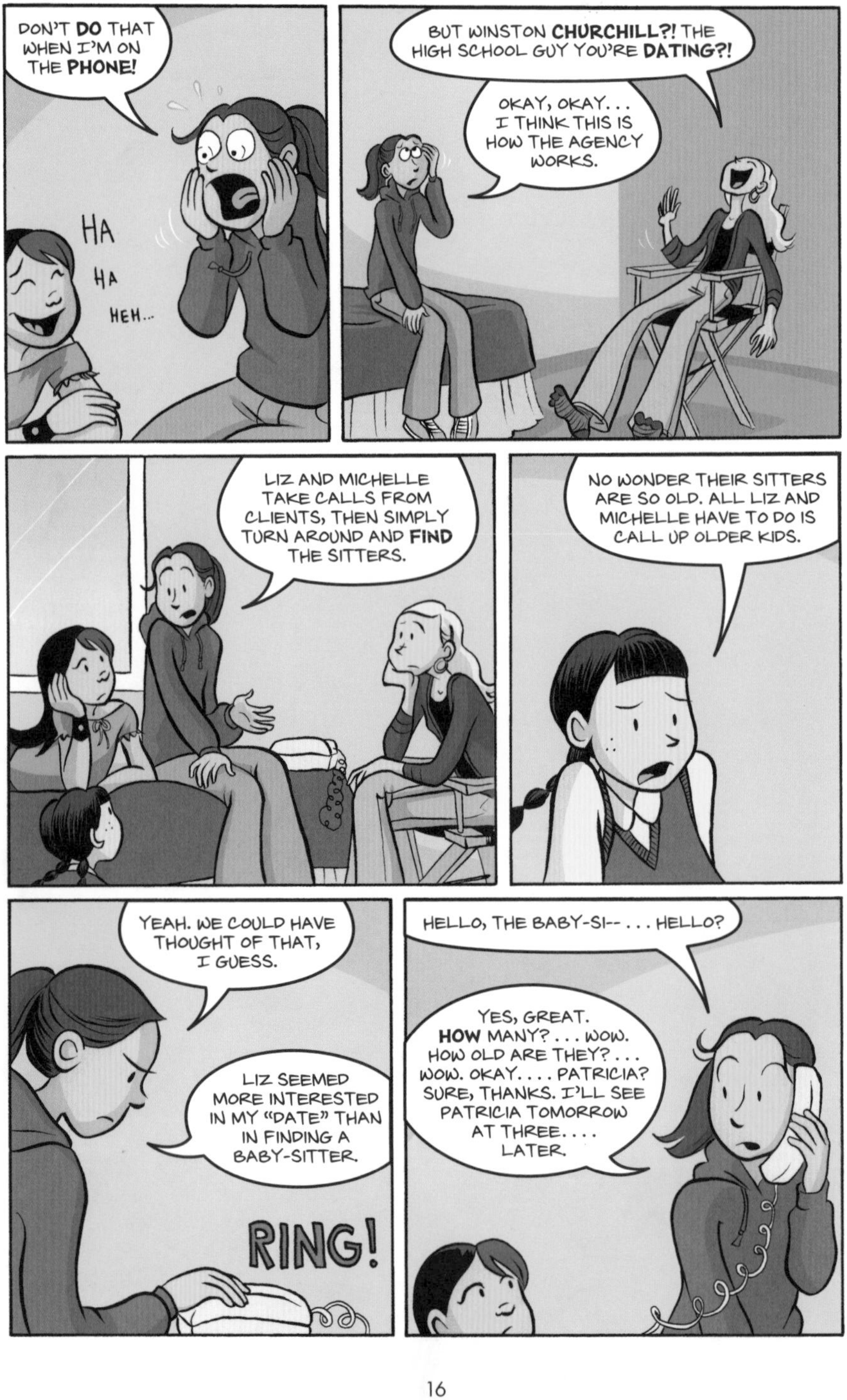
DON'T **DO** THAT WHEN I'M ON THE **PHONE!**
HA
HA
HEH...
BUT WINSTON **CHURCHILL?!** THE HIGH SCHOOL GUY YOU'RE **DATING?!**
OKAY, OKAY... I THINK THIS IS HOW THE AGENCY WORKS.
LIZ AND MICHELLE TAKE CALLS FROM CLIENTS, THEN SIMPLY TURN AROUND AND **FIND** THE SITTERS.
NO WONDER THEIR SITTERS ARE SO OLD. ALL LIZ AND MICHELLE HAVE TO DO IS CALL UP OLDER KIDS.
YEAH. WE COULD HAVE THOUGHT OF THAT, I GUESS.
LIZ SEEMED MORE INTERESTED IN MY "DATE" THAN IN FINDING A BABY-SITTER.
RING!
HELLO, THE BABY-SI-- . . . HELLO?
YES, GREAT. **HOW** MANY? . . . WOW. HOW OLD ARE THEY? . . . WOW. OKAY. . . . PATRICIA? SURE, THANKS. I'LL SEE PATRICIA TOMORROW AT THREE. . . . LATER.

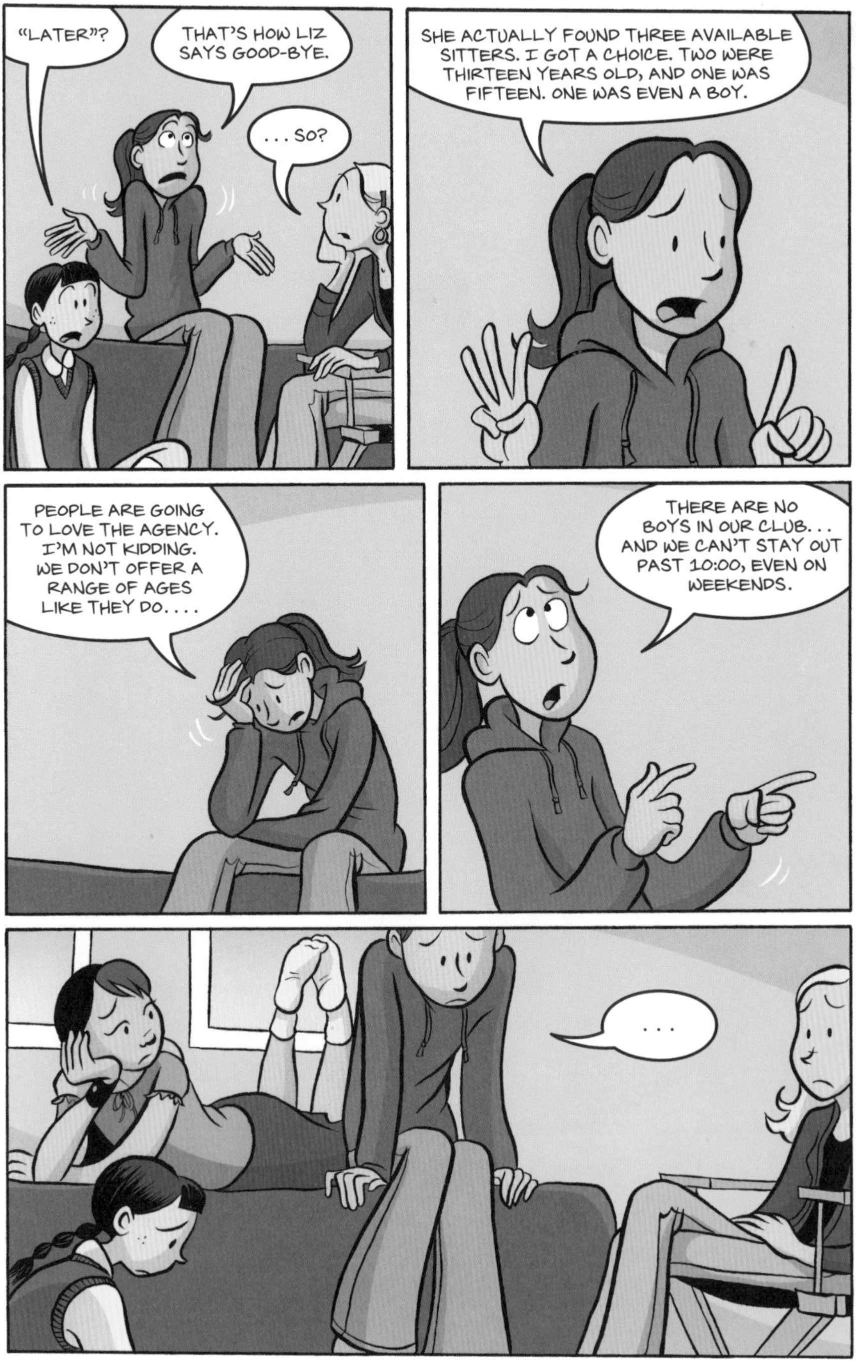
"LATER"?
THAT'S HOW LIZ SAYS GOOD-BYE.
. . . SO?
SHE ACTUALLY FOUND THREE AVAILABLE SITTERS. I GOT A CHOICE. TWO WERE THIRTEEN YEARS OLD, AND ONE WAS FIFTEEN. ONE WAS EVEN A BOY.
PEOPLE ARE GOING TO LOVE THE AGENCY. I'M NOT KIDDING. WE DON'T OFFER A RANGE OF AGES LIKE THEY DO. . . .
THERE ARE NO BOYS IN OUR CLUB. . . AND WE CAN'T STAY OUT PAST 10:00, EVEN ON WEEKENDS.
. . .

STACEY'S DINNER PLATE:

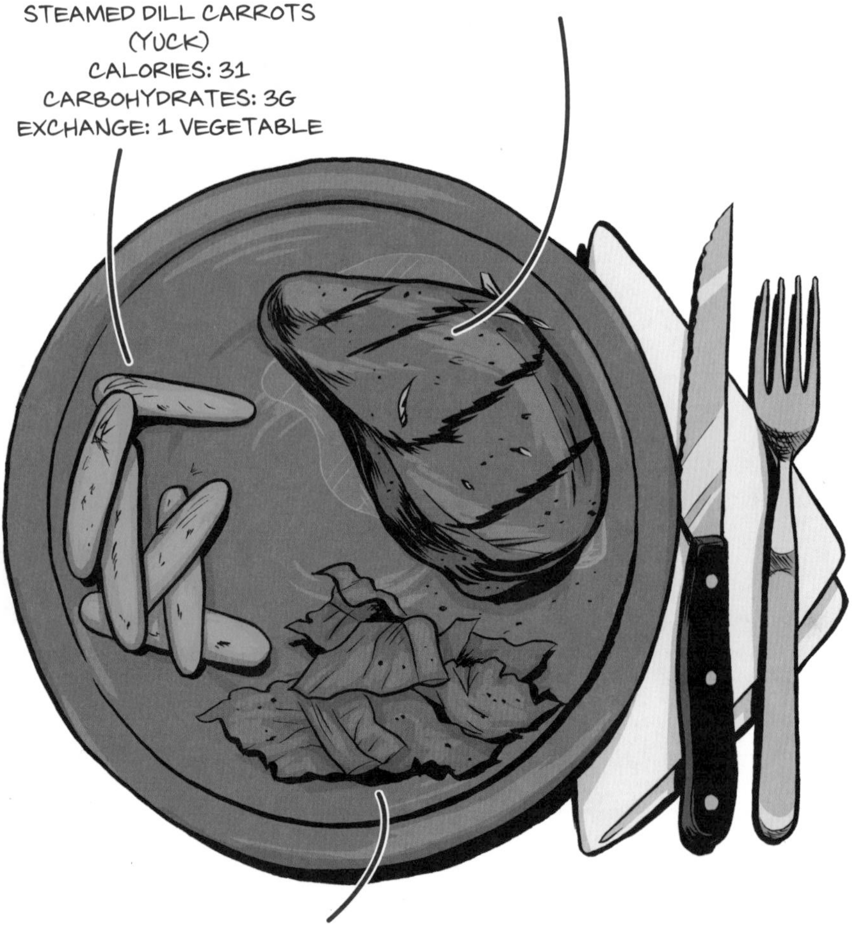
APPLE-GLAZED PORK CHOP
CALORIES: 194
CARBOHYDRATES: 4.8G
EXCHANGE: 1/4 BREAD/STARCH, 1 MEAT
STEAMED DILL CARROTS
(YUCK)
CALORIES: 31
CARBOHYDRATES: 3G
EXCHANGE: 1 VEGETABLE
ROMAINE LETTUCE SALAD
WITH LOW-CAL ITALIAN DRESSING
CALORIES: 39
CARBOHYDRATES: 2.8G
EXCHANGE: 1 VEGETABLE

CHAPTER 3

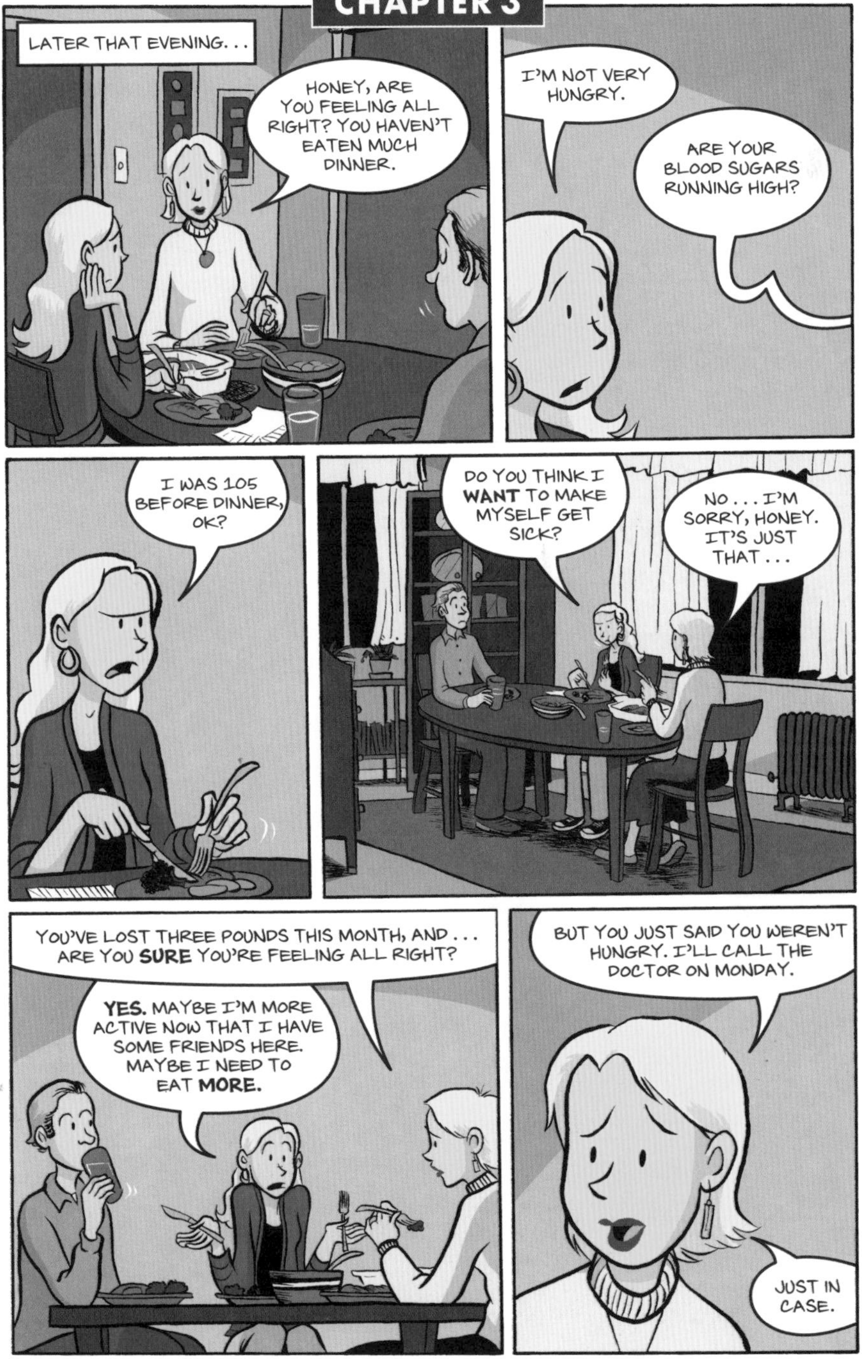
LATER THAT EVENING. . .
HONEY, ARE YOU FEELING ALL RIGHT? YOU HAVEN'T EATEN MUCH DINNER.
I'M NOT VERY HUNGRY.
ARE YOUR BLOOD SUGARS RUNNING HIGH?
I WAS 105 BEFORE DINNER, OK?
DO YOU THINK I **WANT** TO MAKE MYSELF GET SICK?
NO . . . I'M SORRY, HONEY. IT'S JUST THAT . . .
YOU'VE LOST THREE POUNDS THIS MONTH, AND . . . ARE YOU **SURE** YOU'RE FEELING ALL RIGHT?
YES. MAYBE I'M MORE ACTIVE NOW THAT I HAVE SOME FRIENDS HERE. MAYBE I NEED TO EAT **MORE.**
BUT YOU JUST SAID YOU WEREN'T HUNGRY. I'LL CALL THE DOCTOR ON MONDAY.
JUST IN CASE.

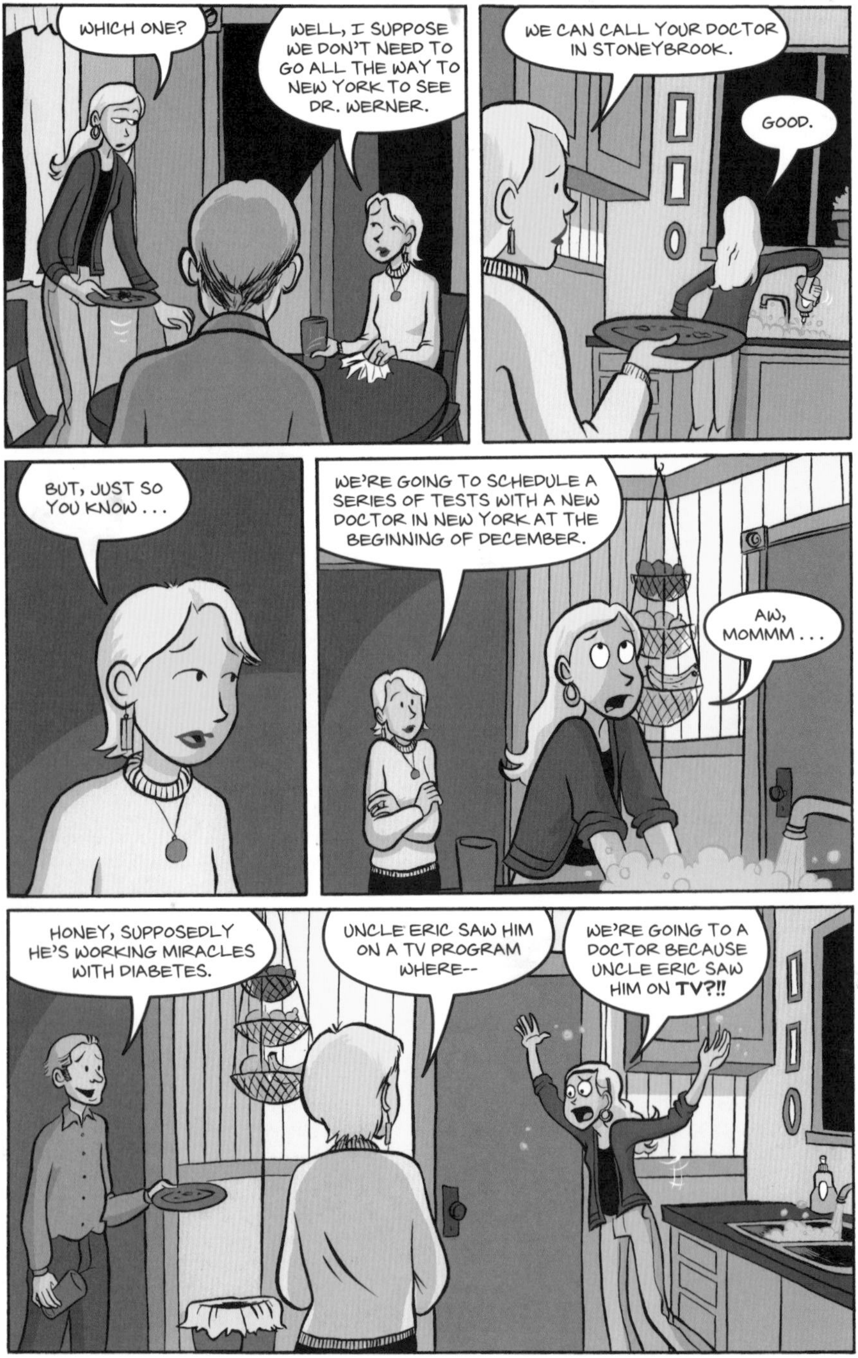
WHICH ONE?
WELL, I SUPPOSE WE DON'T NEED TO GO ALL THE WAY TO NEW YORK TO SEE DR. WERNER.
WE CAN CALL YOUR DOCTOR IN STONEYBROOK.
GOOD.
BUT, JUST SO YOU KNOW . . .
WE'RE GOING TO SCHEDULE A SERIES OF TESTS WITH A NEW DOCTOR IN NEW YORK AT THE BEGINNING OF DECEMBER.
AW, MOMMM . . .
HONEY, SUPPOSEDLY HE'S WORKING MIRACLES WITH DIABETES.
UNCLE ERIC SAW HIM ON A TV PROGRAM WHERE--
WE'RE GOING TO A DOCTOR BECAUSE UNCLE ERIC SAW HIM ON TV?!!

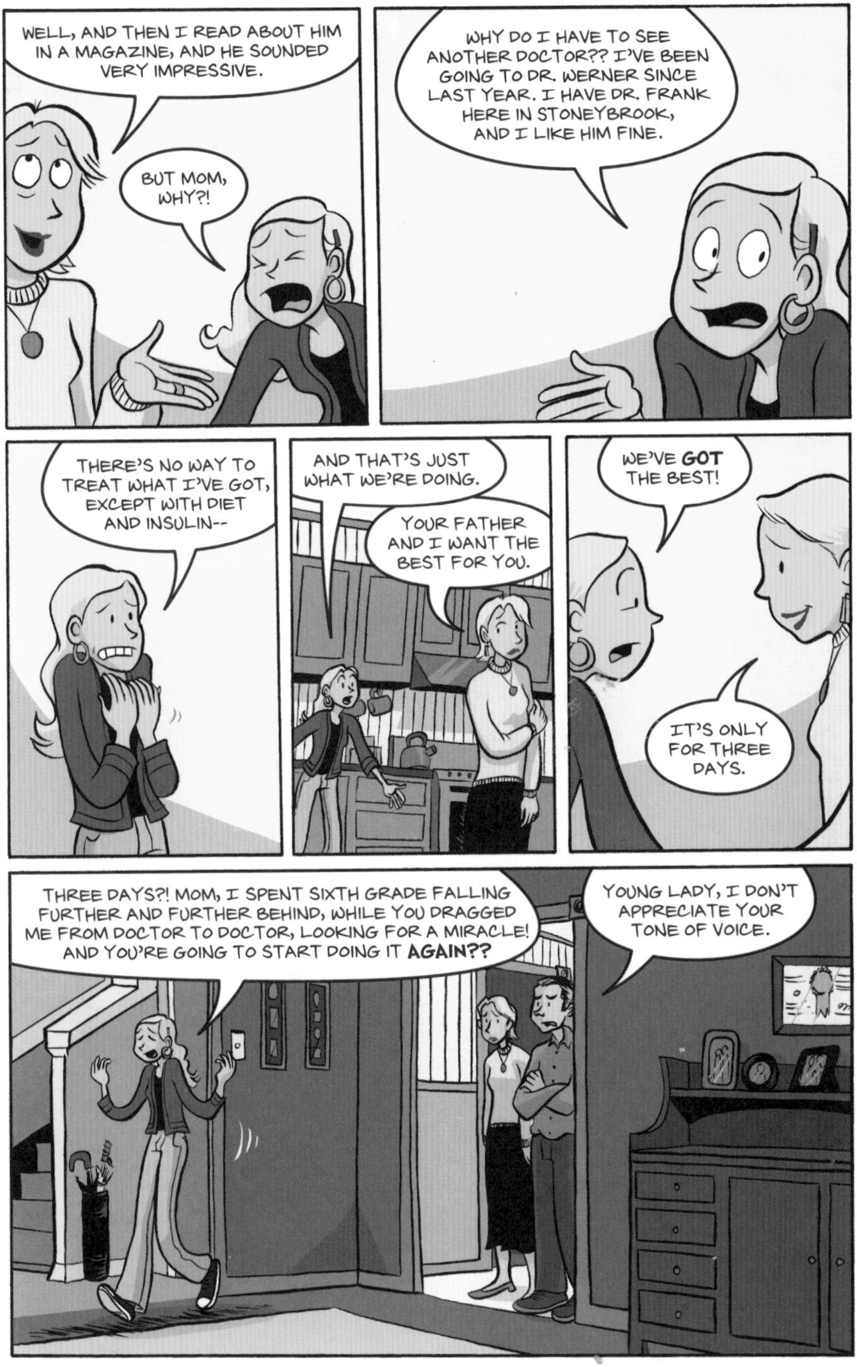
WELL, AND THEN I READ ABOUT HIM IN A MAGAZINE, AND HE SOUNDED VERY IMPRESSIVE.
BUT MOM, WHY?!
WHY DO I HAVE TO SEE ANOTHER DOCTOR?? I'VE BEEN GOING TO DR. WERNER SINCE LAST YEAR. I HAVE DR. FRANK HERE IN STONEYBROOK, AND I LIKE HIM FINE.
THERE'S NO WAY TO TREAT WHAT I'VE GOT, EXCEPT WITH DIET AND INSULIN--
AND THAT'S JUST WHAT WE'RE DOING.
YOUR FATHER AND I WANT THE BEST FOR YOU.
WE'VE **GOT** THE BEST!
IT'S ONLY FOR THREE DAYS.
THREE DAYS?! MOM, I SPENT SIXTH GRADE FALLING FURTHER AND FURTHER BEHIND, WHILE YOU DRAGGED ME FROM DOCTOR TO DOCTOR, LOOKING FOR A MIRACLE! AND YOU'RE GOING TO START DOING IT **AGAIN??**
YOUNG LADY, I DON'T APPRECIATE YOUR TONE OF VOICE.

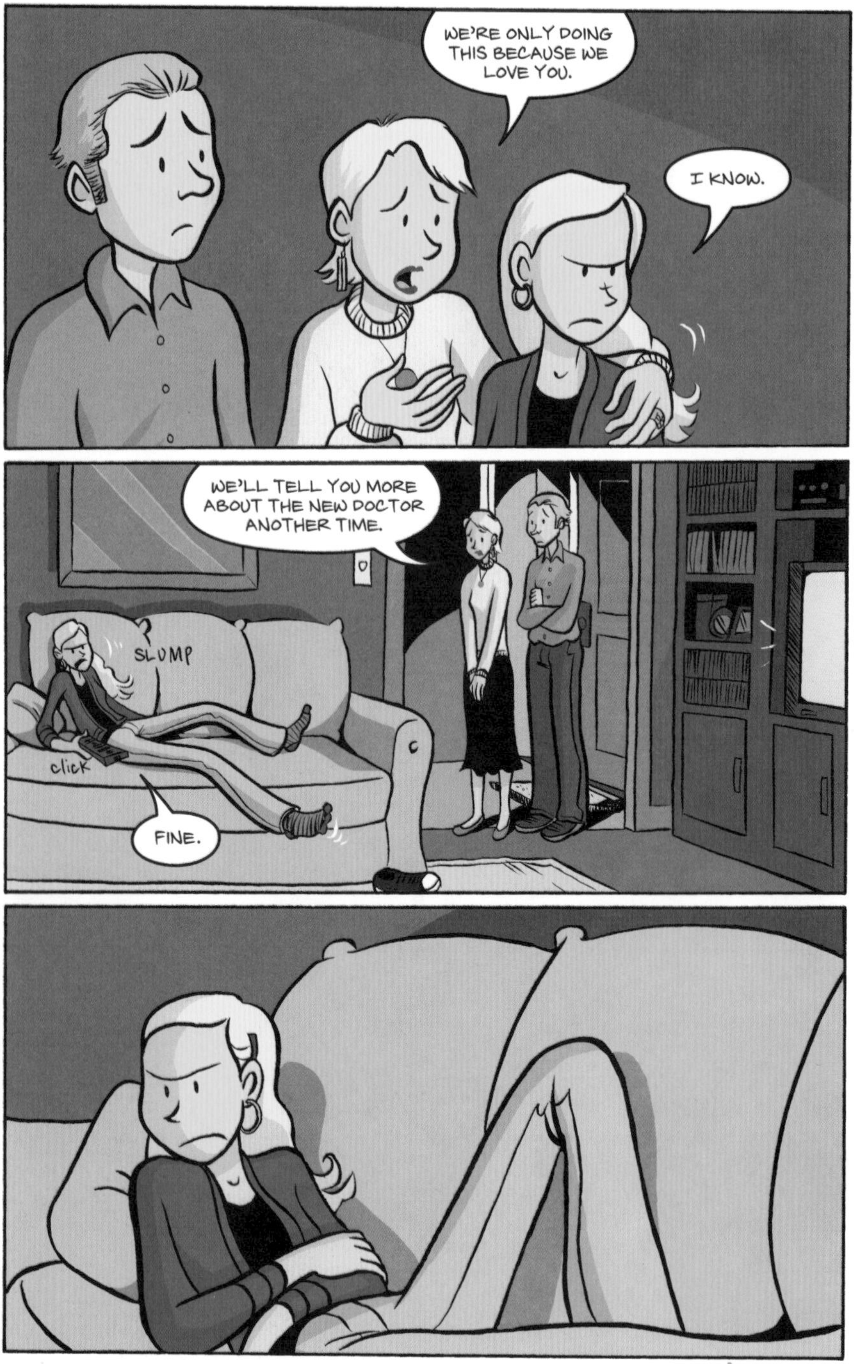
WE'RE ONLY DOING THIS BECAUSE WE LOVE YOU.
I KNOW.
WE'LL TELL YOU MORE ABOUT THE NEW DOCTOR ANOTHER TIME.
SLUMP
click
FINE.

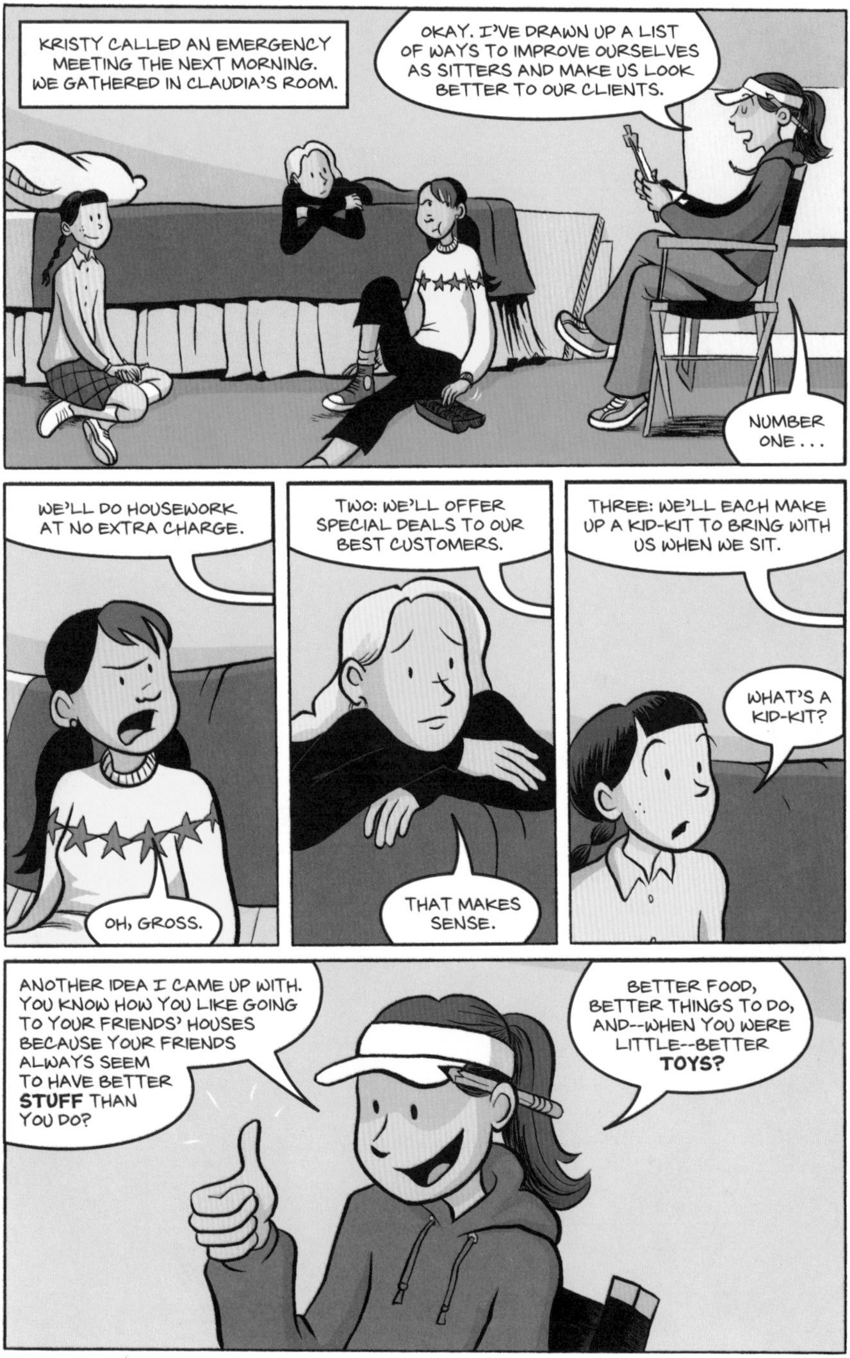
KRISTY CALLED AN EMERGENCY MEETING THE NEXT MORNING. WE GATHERED IN CLAUDIA'S ROOM.
OKAY. I'VE DRAWN UP A LIST OF WAYS TO IMPROVE OURSELVES AS SITTERS AND MAKE US LOOK BETTER TO OUR CLIENTS.
NUMBER ONE . . .
WE'LL DO HOUSEWORK AT NO EXTRA CHARGE.
OH, GROSS.
TWO: WE'LL OFFER SPECIAL DEALS TO OUR BEST CUSTOMERS.
THAT MAKES SENSE.
THREE: WE'LL EACH MAKE UP A KID-KIT TO BRING WITH US WHEN WE SIT.
WHAT'S A KID-KIT?
ANOTHER IDEA I CAME UP WITH. YOU KNOW HOW YOU LIKE GOING TO YOUR FRIENDS' HOUSES BECAUSE YOUR FRIENDS ALWAYS SEEM TO HAVE BETTER **STUFF** THAN YOU DO?
BETTER FOOD, BETTER THINGS TO DO, AND--WHEN YOU WERE LITTLE--BETTER **TOYS?**

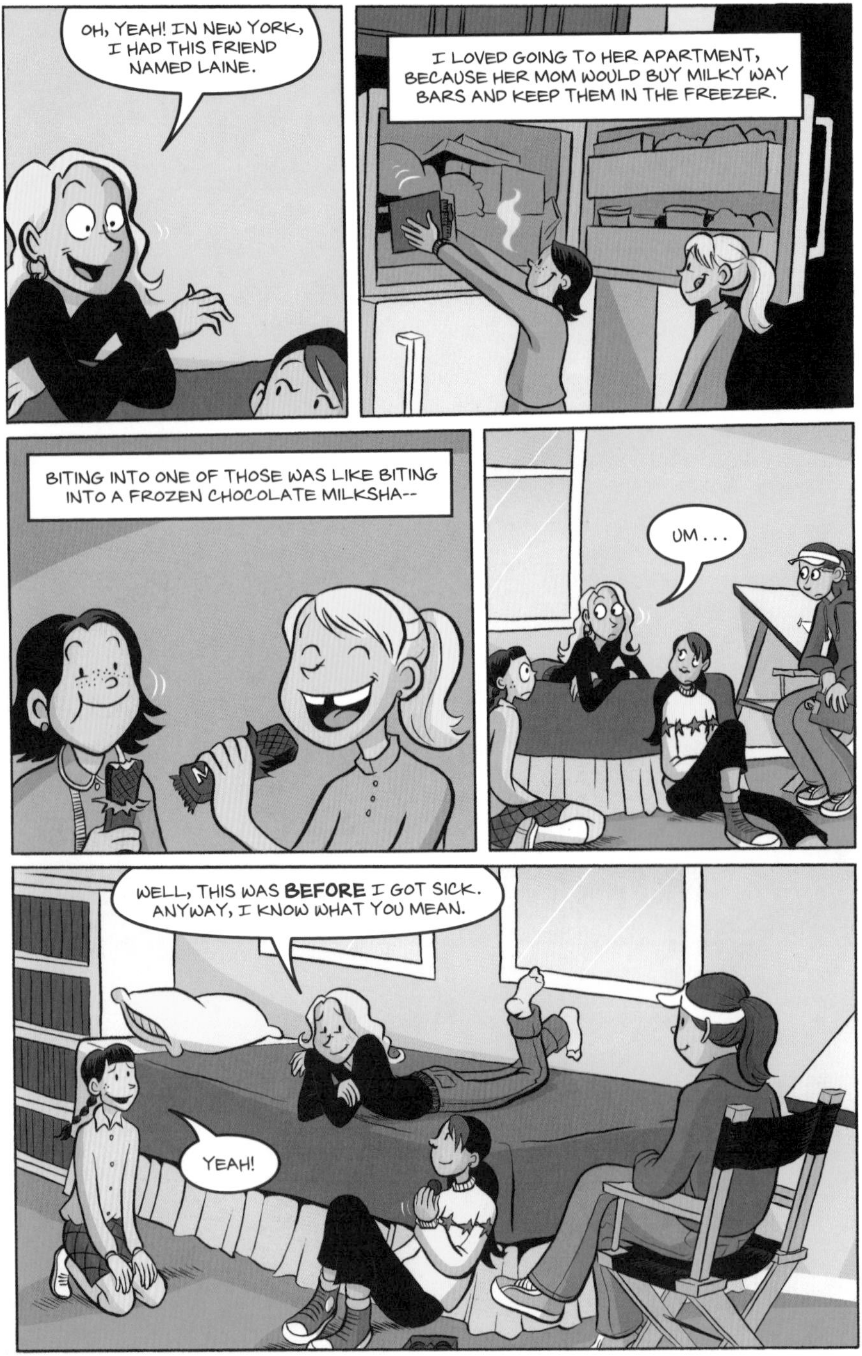
OH, YEAH! IN NEW YORK, I HAD THIS FRIEND NAMED LAINE.
I LOVED GOING TO HER APARTMENT, BECAUSE HER MOM WOULD BUY MILKY WAY BARS AND KEEP THEM IN THE FREEZER.
BITING INTO ONE OF THOSE WAS LIKE BITING INTO A FROZEN CHOCOLATE MILKSHA--
UM . . .
WELL, THIS WAS **BEFORE** I GOT SICK. ANYWAY, I KNOW WHAT YOU MEAN.
YEAH!

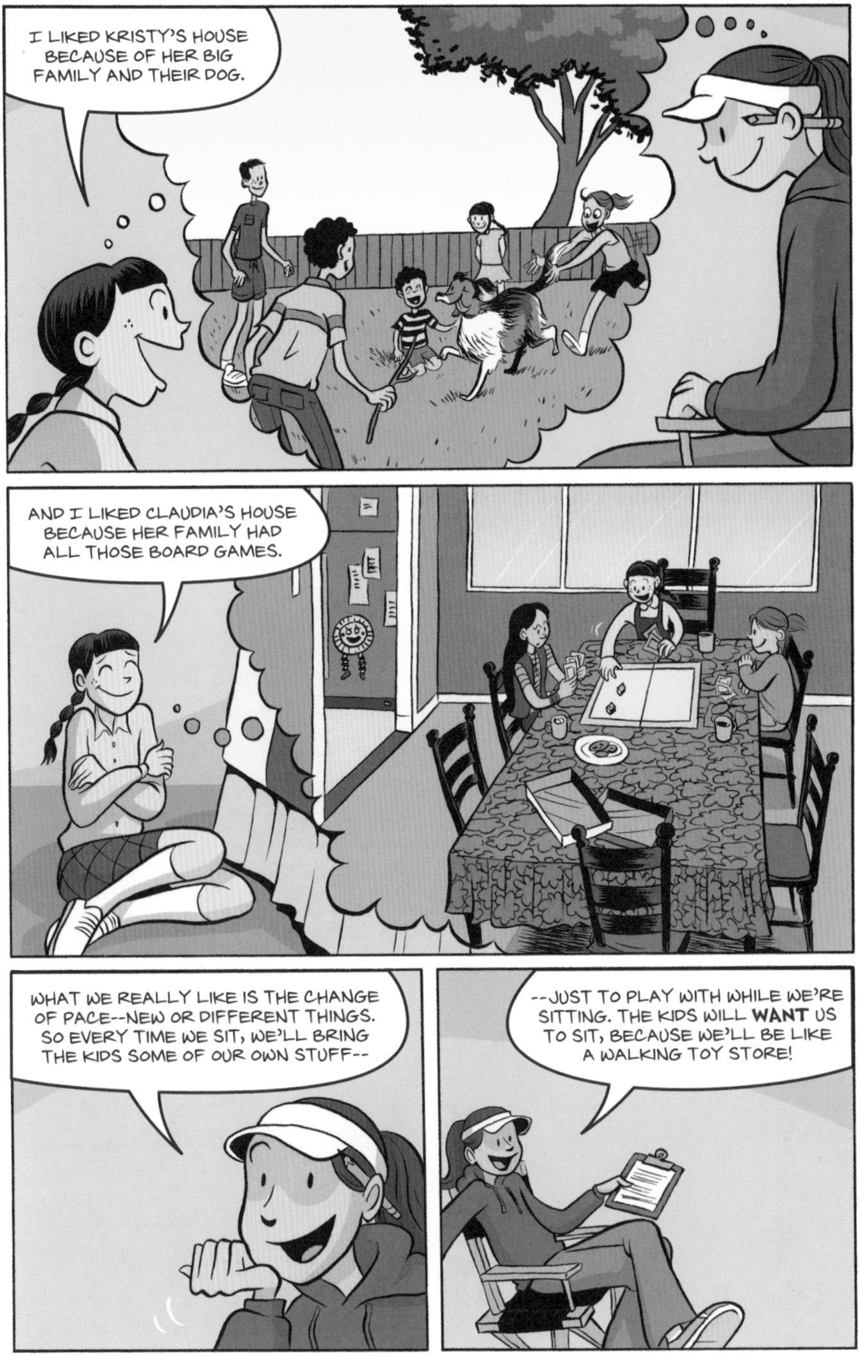
I LIKED KRISTY'S HOUSE BECAUSE OF HER BIG FAMILY AND THEIR DOG.
AND I LIKED CLAUDIA'S HOUSE BECAUSE HER FAMILY HAD ALL THOSE BOARD GAMES.
WHAT WE REALLY LIKE IS THE CHANGE OF PACE--NEW OR DIFFERENT THINGS. SO EVERY TIME WE SIT, WE'LL BRING THE KIDS SOME OF OUR OWN STUFF--
--JUST TO PLAY WITH WHILE WE'RE SITTING. THE KIDS WILL **WANT** US TO SIT, BECAUSE WE'LL BE LIKE A WALKING TOY STORE!

27

28

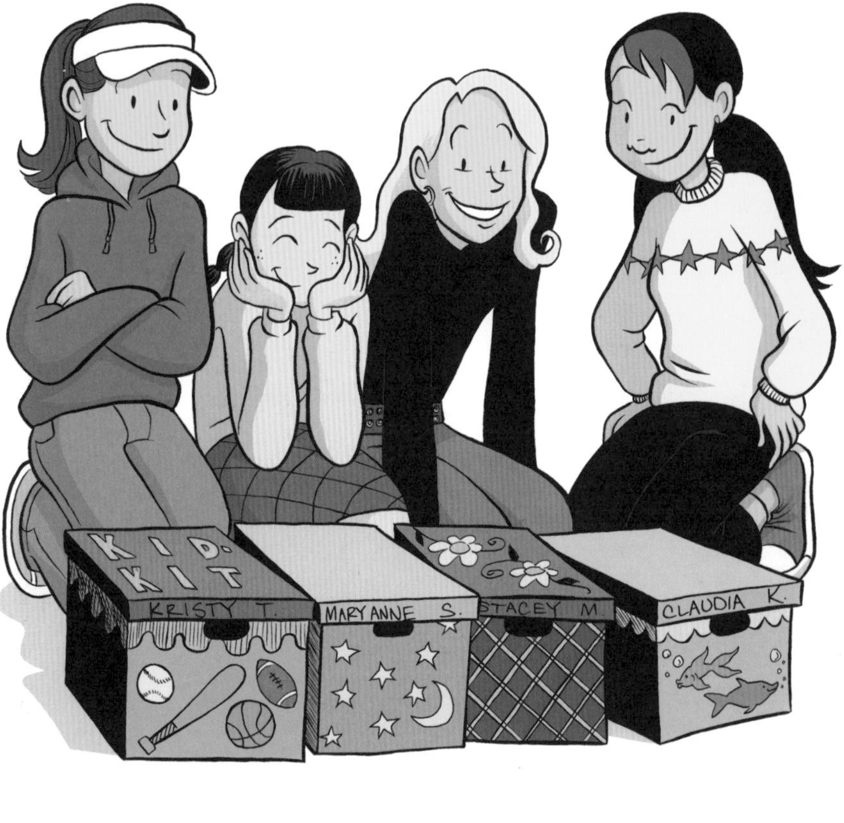
KID-KIT
KRISTY T.
MARYANNE S.
STACEY M.
CLAUDIA K.

November 10

   Monday I had a sitting job for Charlotte Johanssen.
I love sitting for Charlotte, she's one of my very
favorite kids. And her mother, Dr. Johanssen, is a Doctor
at Stoneybrook Medical Center, so I like talking to
her — she always asks me how I'm doing and how
I feel about my treatments. Today was no different,
except for what happened near the end of
the afternoon ...

                        Stacey

CHAPTER 4

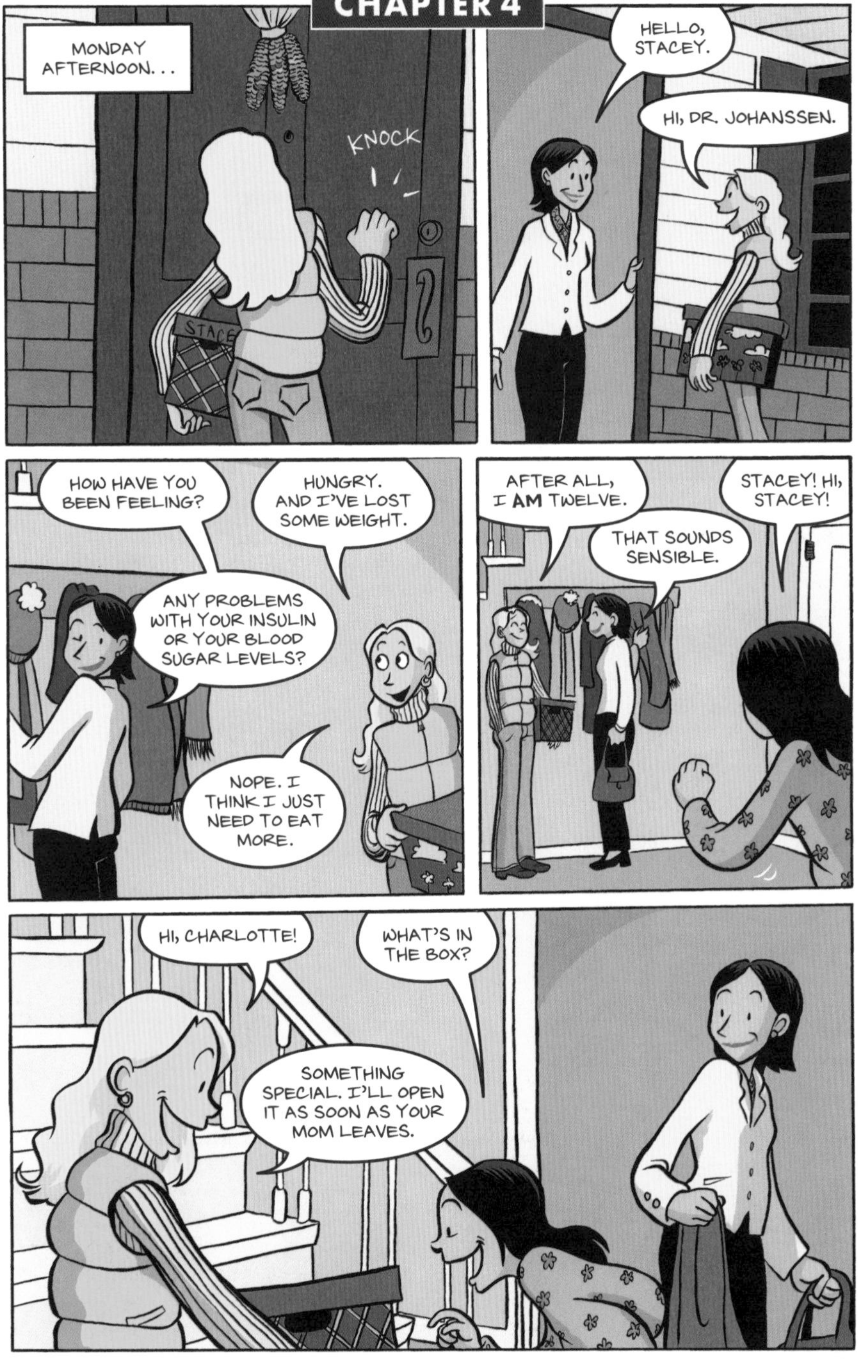

MONDAY AFTERNOON. . .
KNOCK
STACE
HELLO, STACEY.
HI, DR. JOHANSSEN.
HOW HAVE YOU BEEN FEELING?
HUNGRY. AND I'VE LOST SOME WEIGHT.
ANY PROBLEMS WITH YOUR INSULIN OR YOUR BLOOD SUGAR LEVELS?
NOPE. I THINK I JUST NEED TO EAT MORE.
AFTER ALL, I **AM** TWELVE.
THAT SOUNDS SENSIBLE.
STACEY! HI, STACEY!
HI, CHARLOTTE!
WHAT'S IN THE BOX?
SOMETHING SPECIAL. I'LL OPEN IT AS SOON AS YOUR MOM LEAVES.

32

33

34

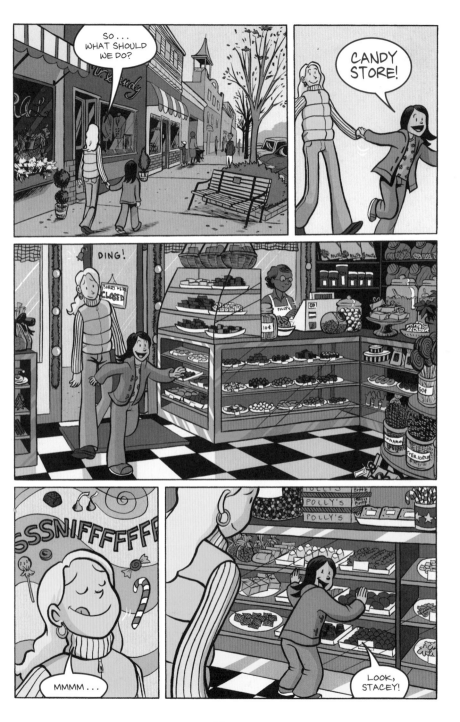

35

36

37

40

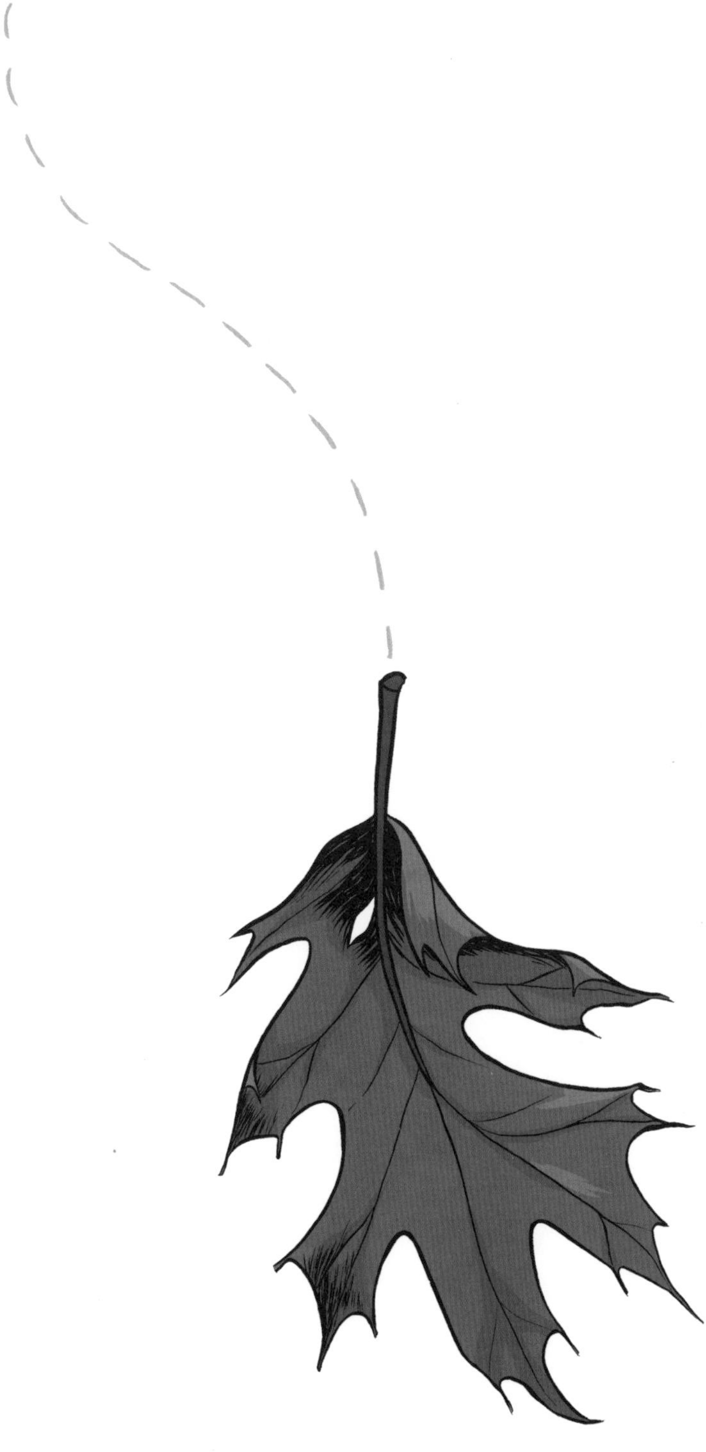

Sunday, November 23

It is just one week since Liz Lewis and Michelle Patterson sent around their fliers. Usually, our club gets about fourteen or fifteen jobs a week. Since last Monday, we've had <u>SEVEN</u>. That's why I'm writing in our notebook. This book is supposed to be a diary of our baby-sitting jobs, so each of us can write up our problems and experiences for the other club members to read. But the Baby-sitters Agency is the biggest problem we've ever had, and I plan to keep track of it in our notebook.

We better do something fast.

— Kristy

45

46

47

48

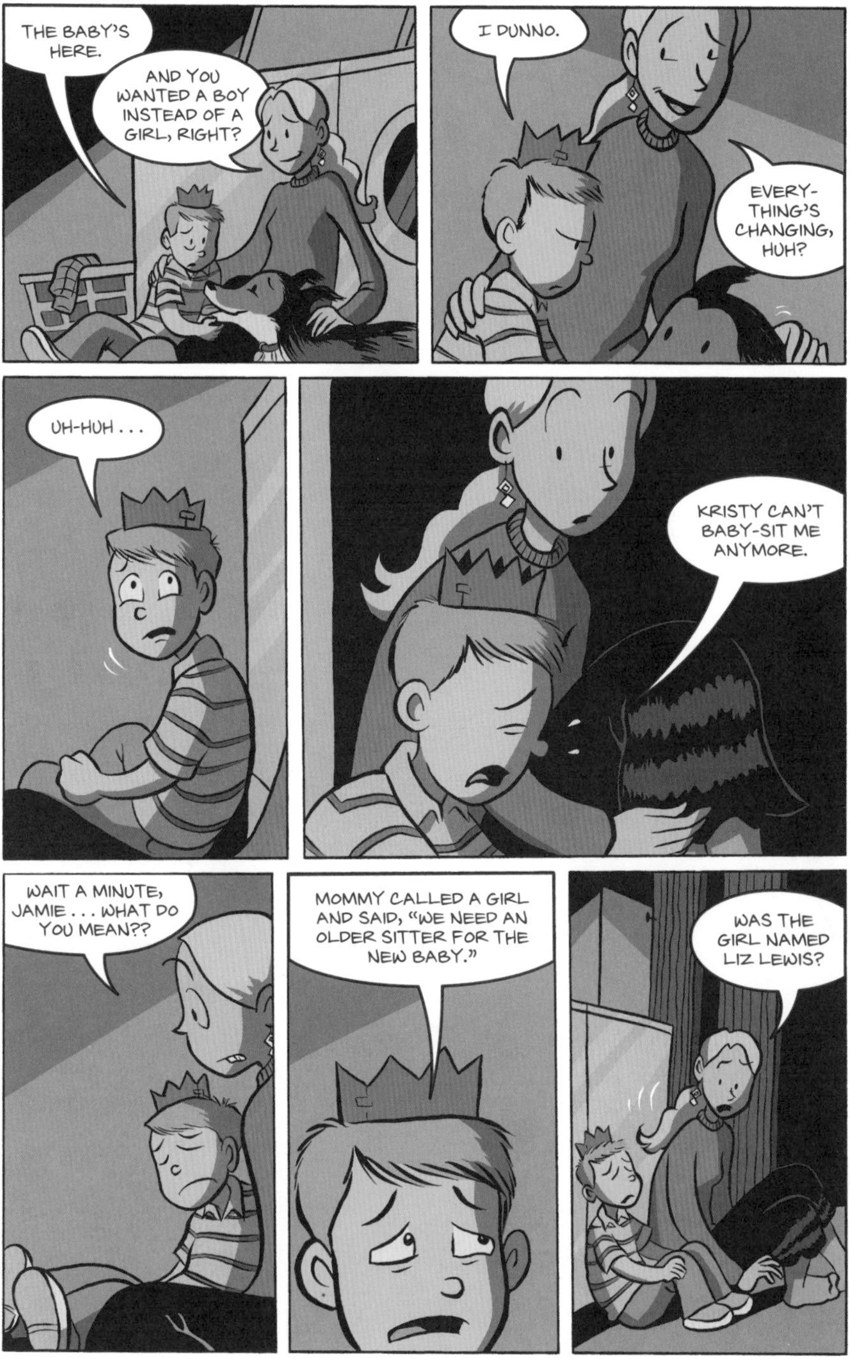

THE BABY'S HERE.
AND YOU WANTED A BOY INSTEAD OF A GIRL, RIGHT?
I DUNNO.
EVERY-THING'S CHANGING, HUH?
UH-HUH . . .
KRISTY CAN'T BABY-SIT ME ANYMORE.
WAIT A MINUTE, JAMIE . . . WHAT DO YOU MEAN??
MOMMY CALLED A GIRL AND SAID, "WE NEED AN OLDER SITTER FOR THE NEW BABY."
WAS THE GIRL NAMED LIZ LEWIS?

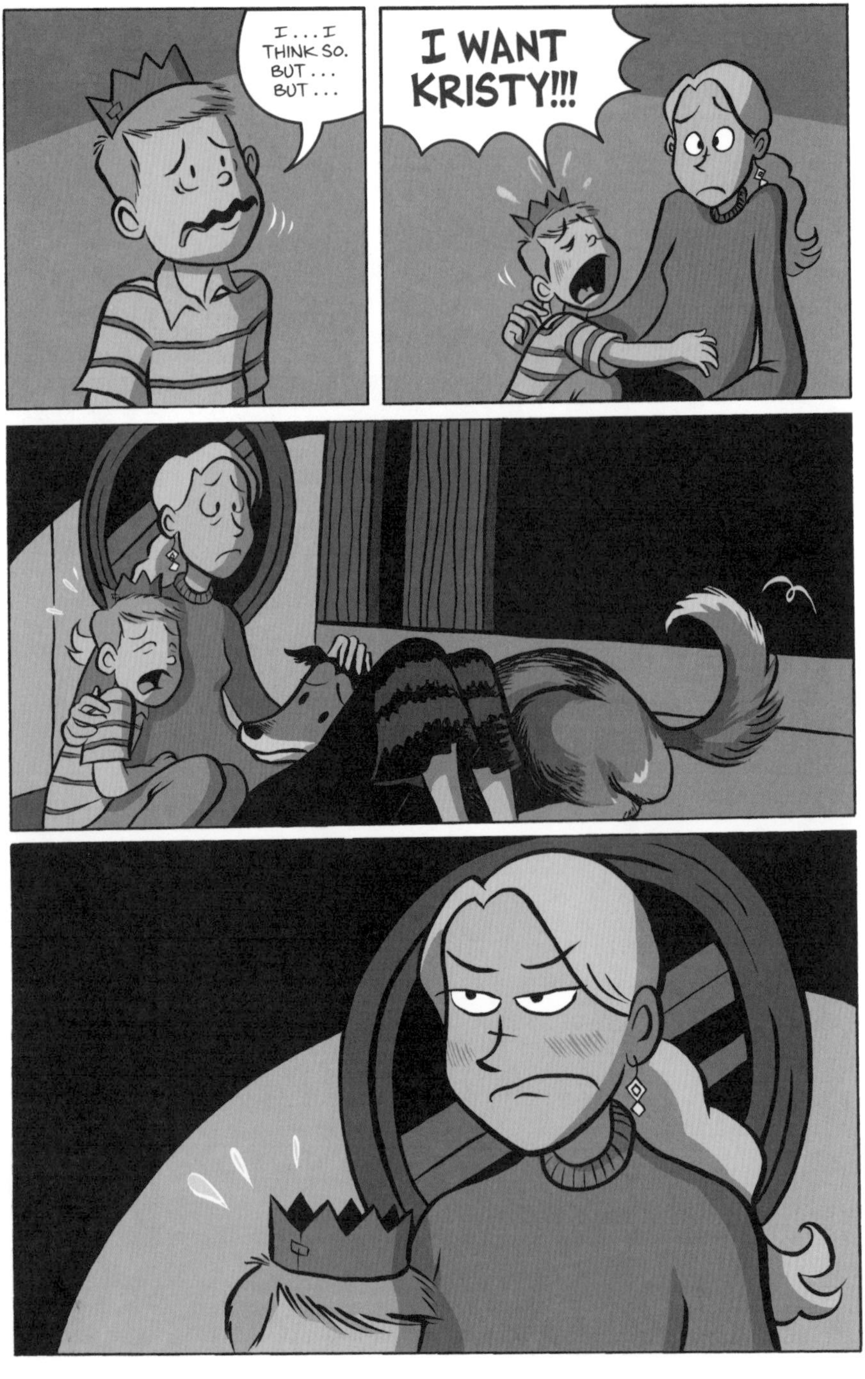
I . . . I THINK SO. BUT . . . BUT . . .
I WANT KRISTY!!!

CHAPTER 6

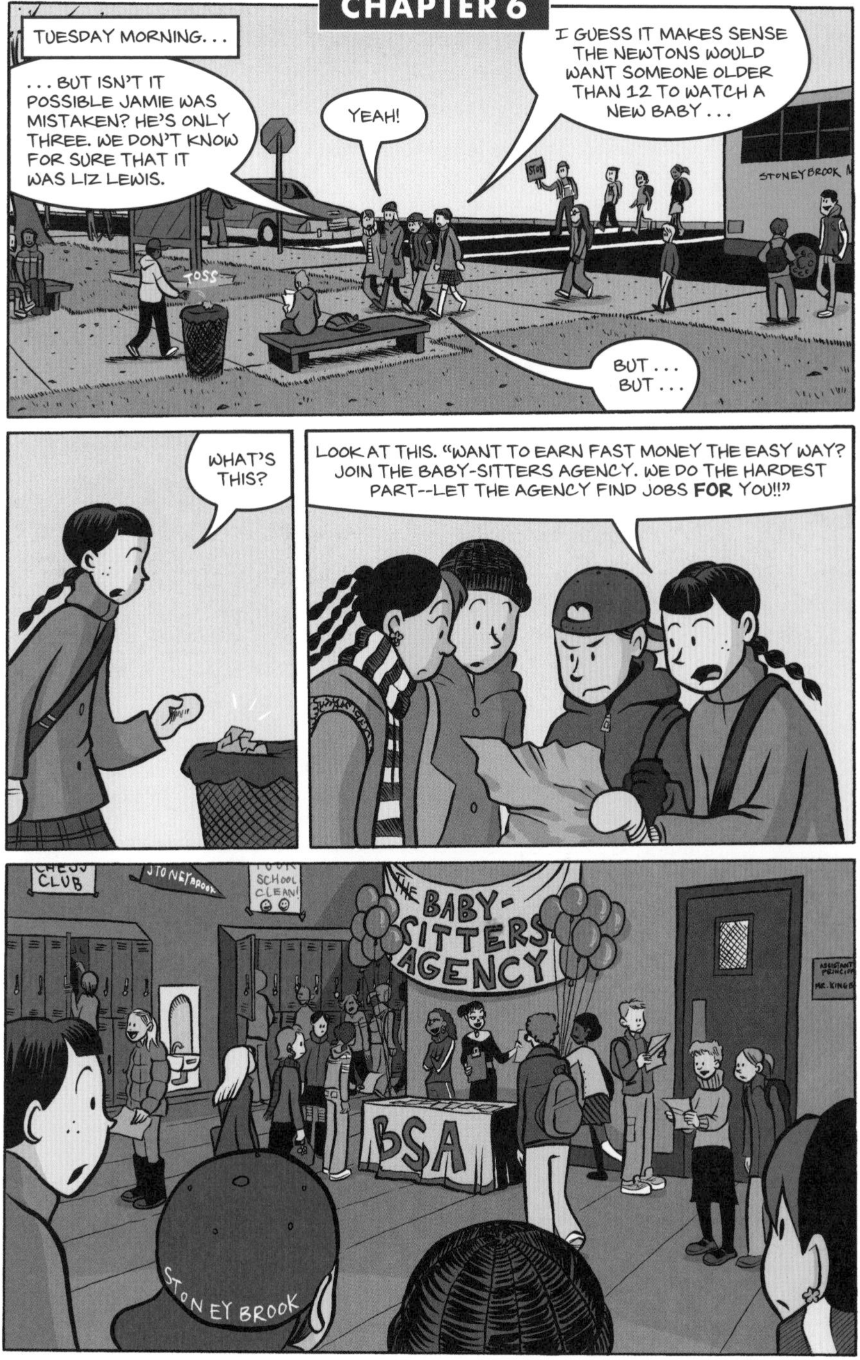
TUESDAY MORNING. . .
. . . BUT ISN'T IT POSSIBLE JAMIE WAS MISTAKEN? HE'S ONLY THREE. WE DON'T KNOW FOR SURE THAT IT WAS LIZ LEWIS.
YEAH!
I GUESS IT MAKES SENSE THE NEWTONS WOULD WANT SOMEONE OLDER THAN 12 TO WATCH A NEW BABY . . .
TOSS
BUT . . . BUT . . .
WHAT'S THIS?
LOOK AT THIS. "WANT TO EARN FAST MONEY THE EASY WAY? JOIN THE BABY-SITTERS AGENCY. WE DO THE HARDEST PART--LET THE AGENCY FIND JOBS **FOR** YOU!!"
CLUB
STONEYBROOK
SCHOOL CLEAN!
THE BABY-SITTERS AGENCY
BSA
STONEY BROOK

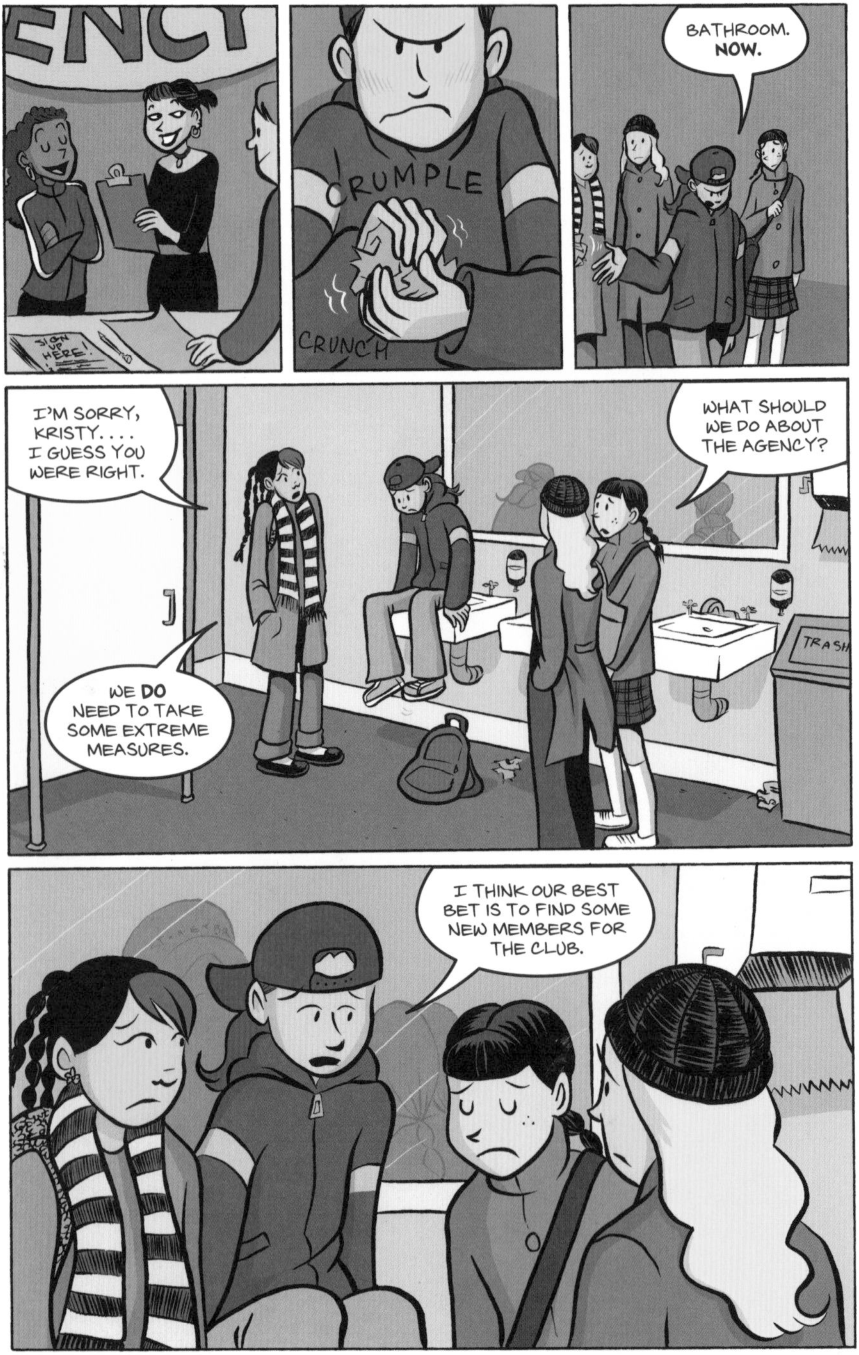
ENCY
SIGN UP HERE!
CRUMPLE
CRUNCH
BATHROOM. **NOW.**
I'M SORRY, KRISTY.... I GUESS YOU WERE RIGHT.
WHAT SHOULD WE DO ABOUT THE AGENCY?
WE **DO** NEED TO TAKE SOME EXTREME MEASURES.
TRASH
I THINK OUR BEST BET IS TO FIND SOME NEW MEMBERS FOR THE CLUB.

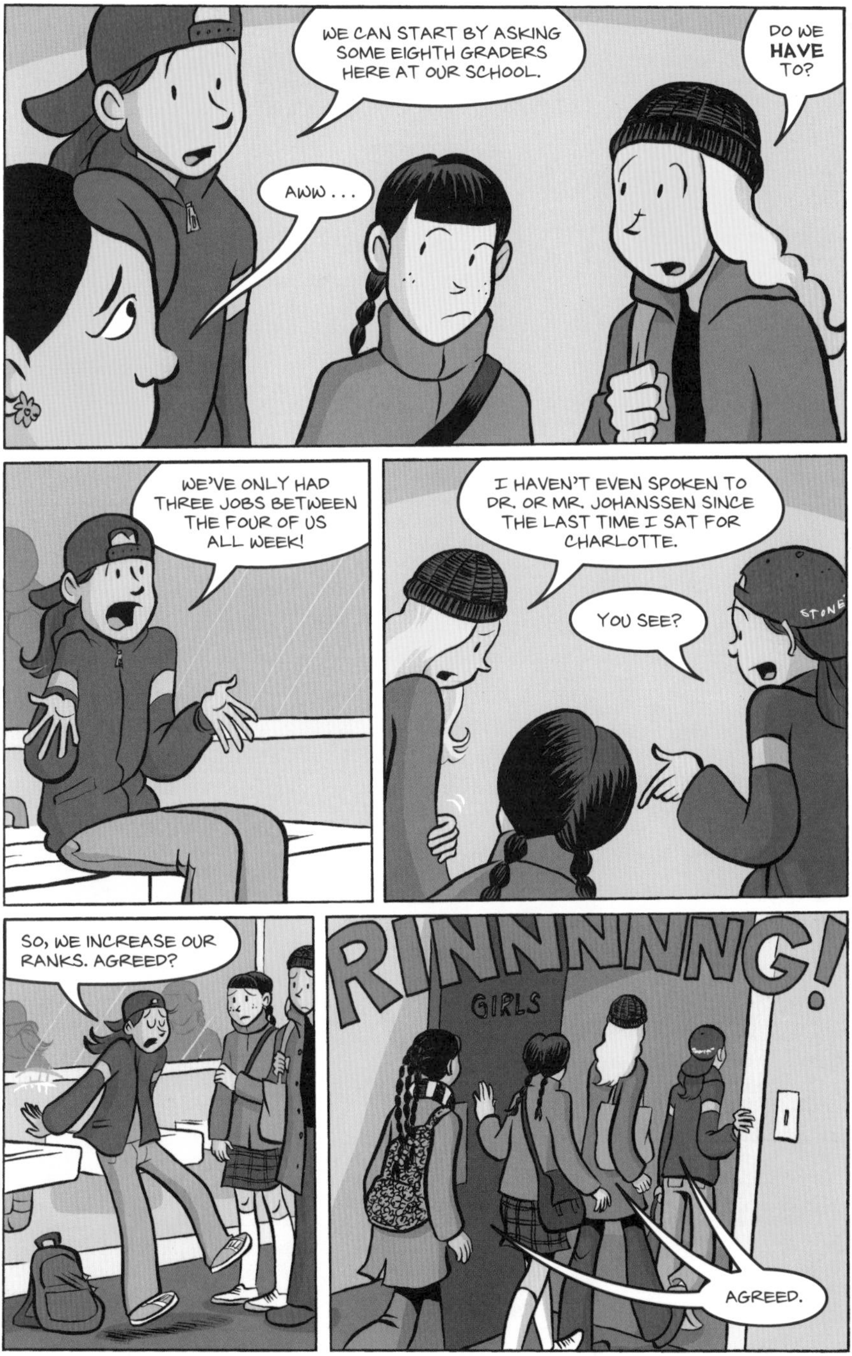

WE CAN START BY ASKING SOME EIGHTH GRADERS HERE AT OUR SCHOOL.
AWW . . .
DO WE **HAVE** TO?
WE'VE ONLY HAD THREE JOBS BETWEEN THE FOUR OF US ALL WEEK!
I HAVEN'T EVEN SPOKEN TO DR. OR MR. JOHANSSEN SINCE THE LAST TIME I SAT FOR CHARLOTTE.
YOU SEE?
STONE
SO, WE INCREASE OUR RANKS. AGREED?
RINNNNNG!
GIRLS
AGREED.

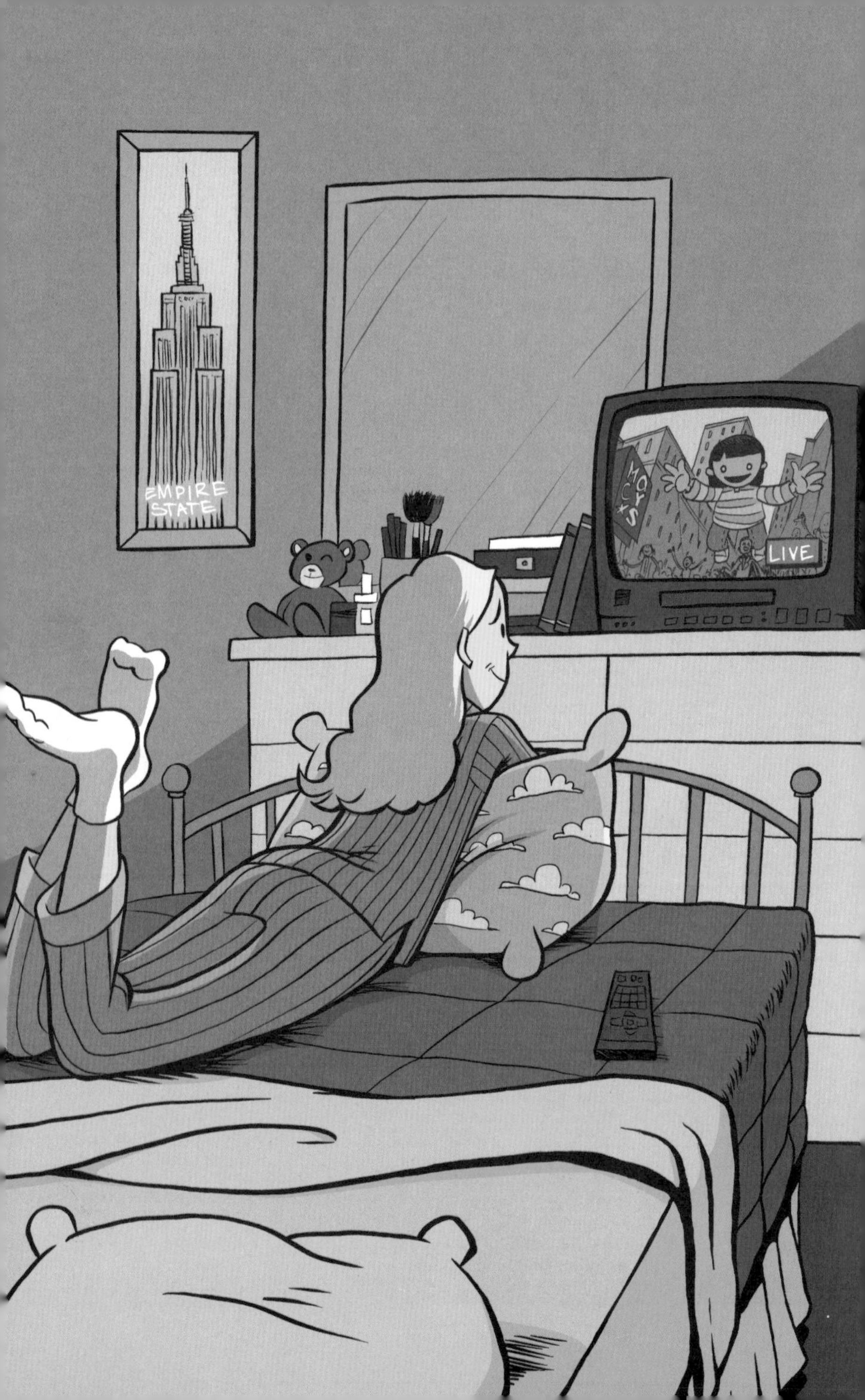

EMPIRE STATE
MACY*S
LIVE

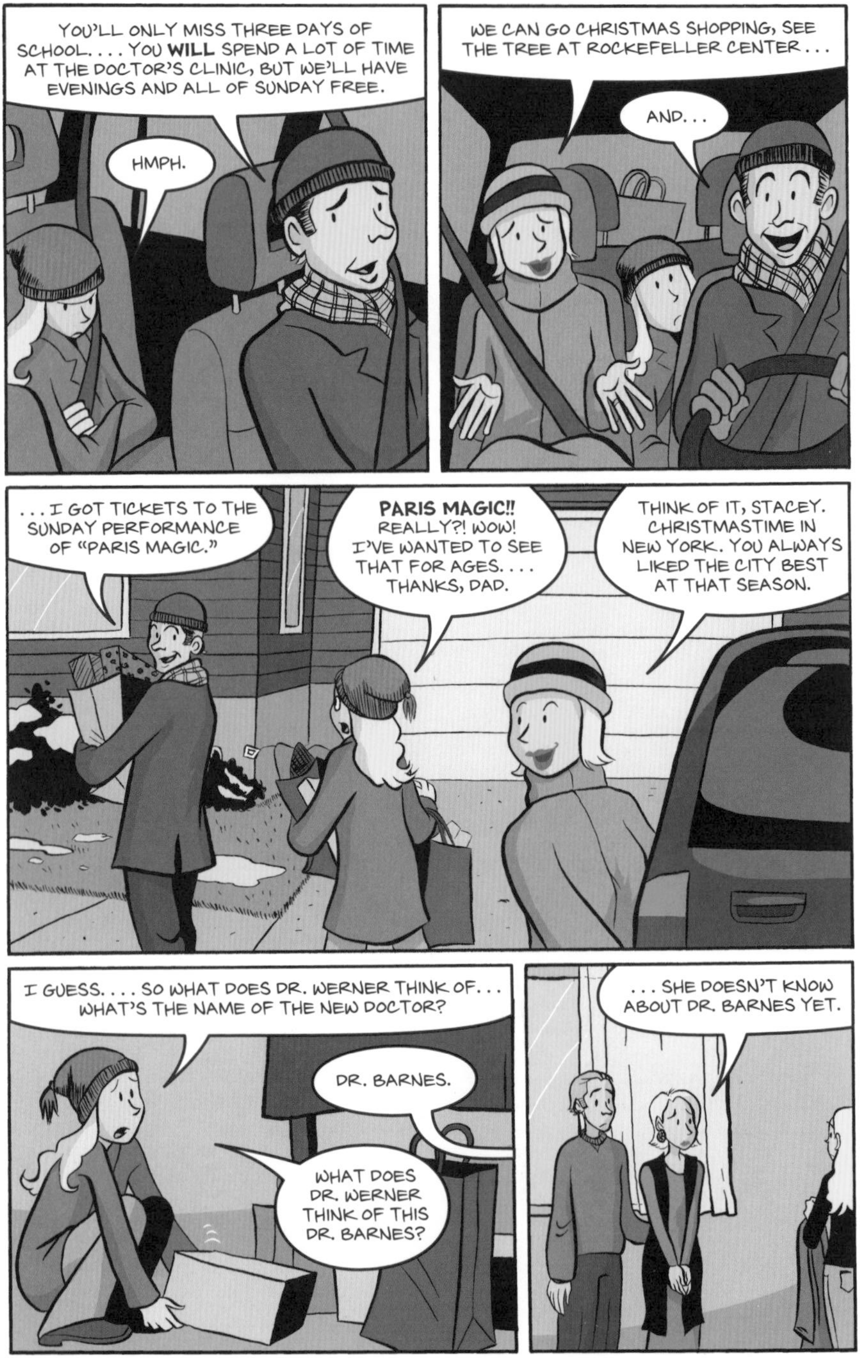
YOU'LL ONLY MISS THREE DAYS OF SCHOOL. . . . YOU **WILL** SPEND A LOT OF TIME AT THE DOCTOR'S CLINIC, BUT WE'LL HAVE EVENINGS AND ALL OF SUNDAY FREE.
HMPH.
WE CAN GO CHRISTMAS SHOPPING, SEE THE TREE AT ROCKEFELLER CENTER . . .
AND. . .
. . . I GOT TICKETS TO THE SUNDAY PERFORMANCE OF "PARIS MAGIC."
PARIS MAGIC!! REALLY?! WOW! I'VE WANTED TO SEE THAT FOR AGES. . . . THANKS, DAD.
THINK OF IT, STACEY. CHRISTMASTIME IN NEW YORK. YOU ALWAYS LIKED THE CITY BEST AT THAT SEASON.
I GUESS. . . . SO WHAT DOES DR. WERNER THINK OF. . . WHAT'S THE NAME OF THE NEW DOCTOR?
DR. BARNES.
WHAT DOES DR. WERNER THINK OF THIS DR. BARNES?
. . . SHE DOESN'T KNOW ABOUT DR. BARNES YET.

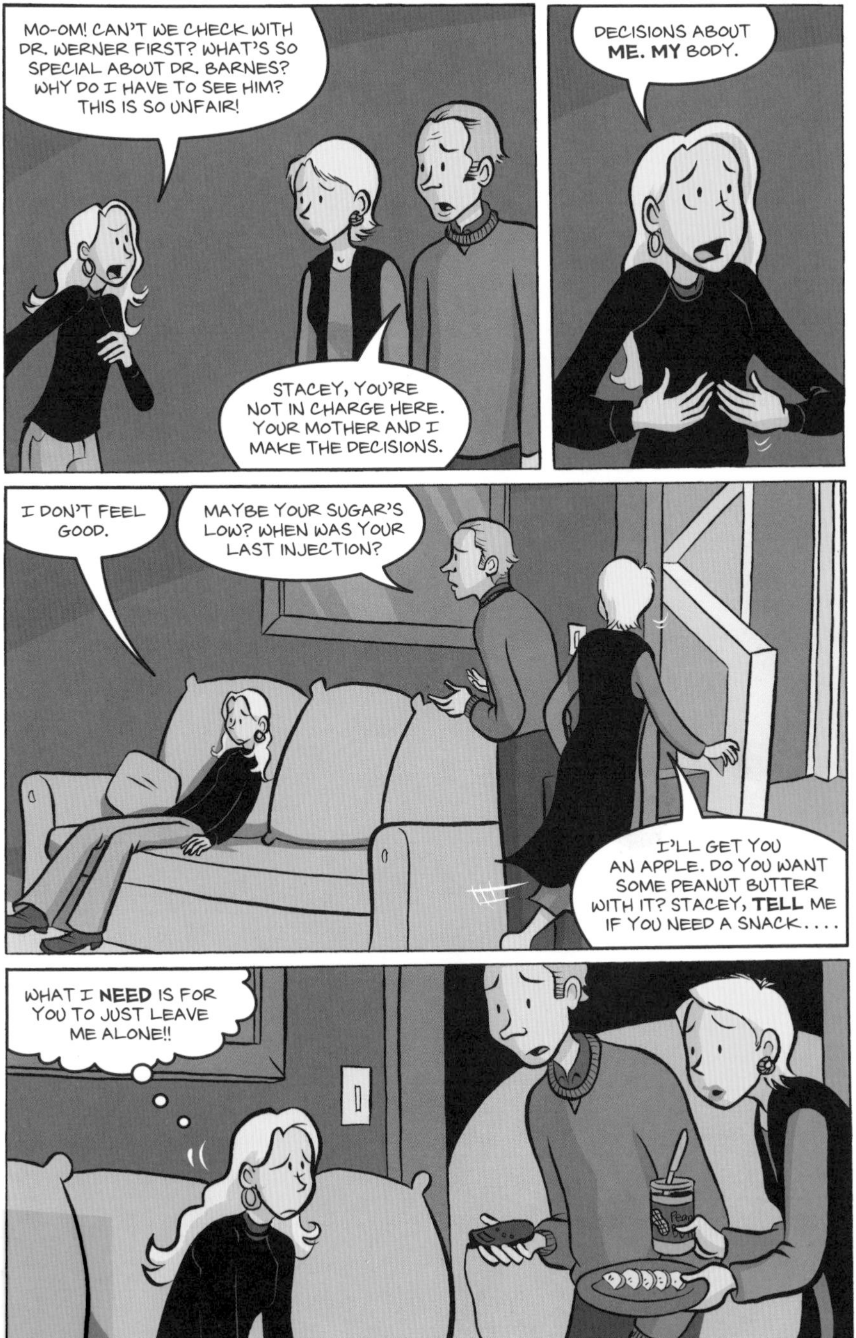
MO-OM! CAN'T WE CHECK WITH DR. WERNER FIRST? WHAT'S SO SPECIAL ABOUT DR. BARNES? WHY DO I HAVE TO SEE HIM? THIS IS SO UNFAIR!
STACEY, YOU'RE NOT IN CHARGE HERE. YOUR MOTHER AND I MAKE THE DECISIONS.
DECISIONS ABOUT **ME. MY** BODY.
I DON'T FEEL GOOD.
MAYBE YOUR SUGAR'S LOW? WHEN WAS YOUR LAST INJECTION?
I'LL GET YOU AN APPLE. DO YOU WANT SOME PEANUT BUTTER WITH IT? STACEY, **TELL** ME IF YOU NEED A SNACK. . . .
WHAT I **NEED** IS FOR YOU TO JUST LEAVE ME ALONE!!

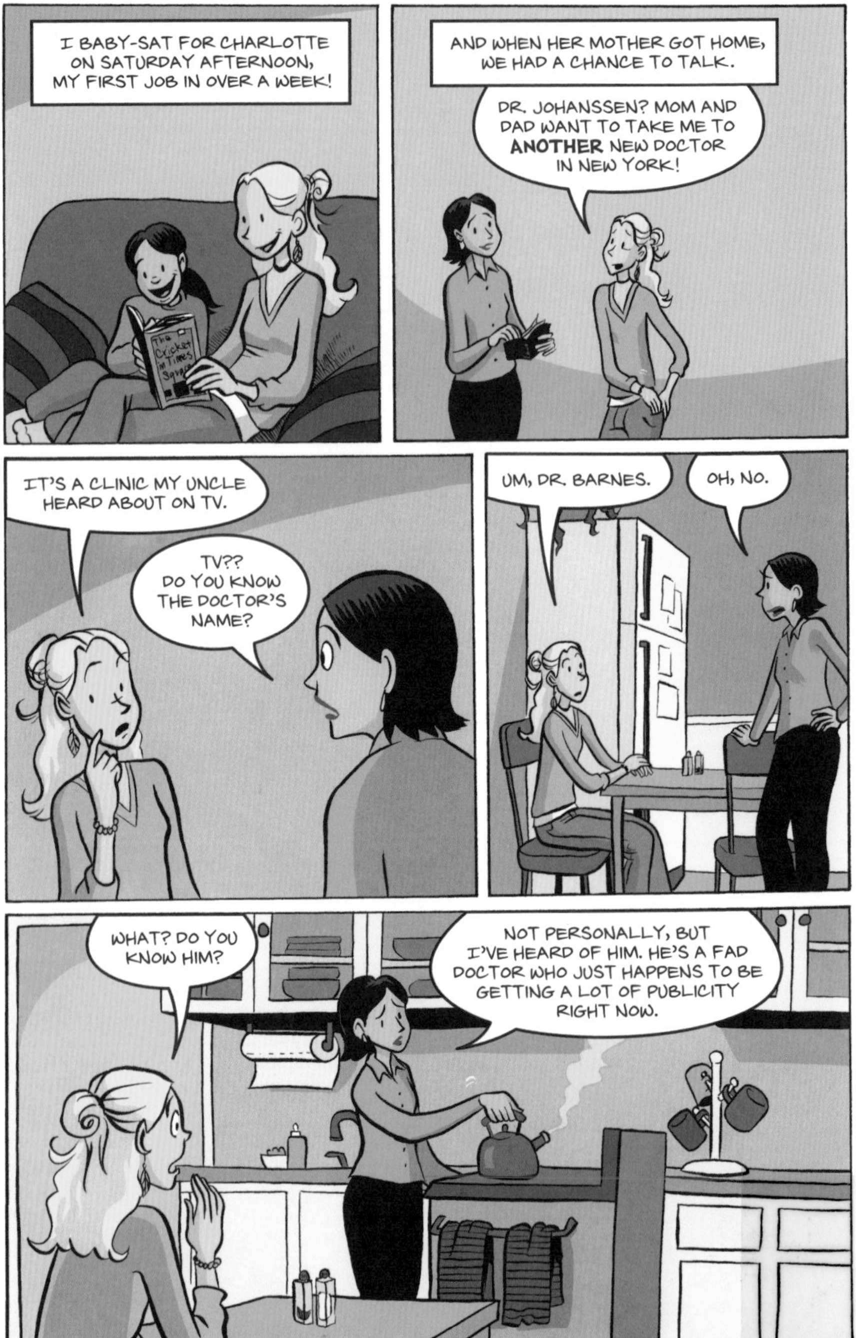
I BABY-SAT FOR CHARLOTTE ON SATURDAY AFTERNOON, MY FIRST JOB IN OVER A WEEK!
The Cricket in Times Square
AND WHEN HER MOTHER GOT HOME, WE HAD A CHANCE TO TALK.
DR. JOHANSSEN? MOM AND DAD WANT TO TAKE ME TO **ANOTHER** NEW DOCTOR IN NEW YORK!
IT'S A CLINIC MY UNCLE HEARD ABOUT ON TV.
TV?? DO YOU KNOW THE DOCTOR'S NAME?
UM, DR. BARNES.
OH, NO.
WHAT? DO YOU KNOW HIM?
NOT PERSONALLY, BUT I'VE HEARD OF HIM. HE'S A FAD DOCTOR WHO JUST HAPPENS TO BE GETTING A LOT OF PUBLICITY RIGHT NOW.

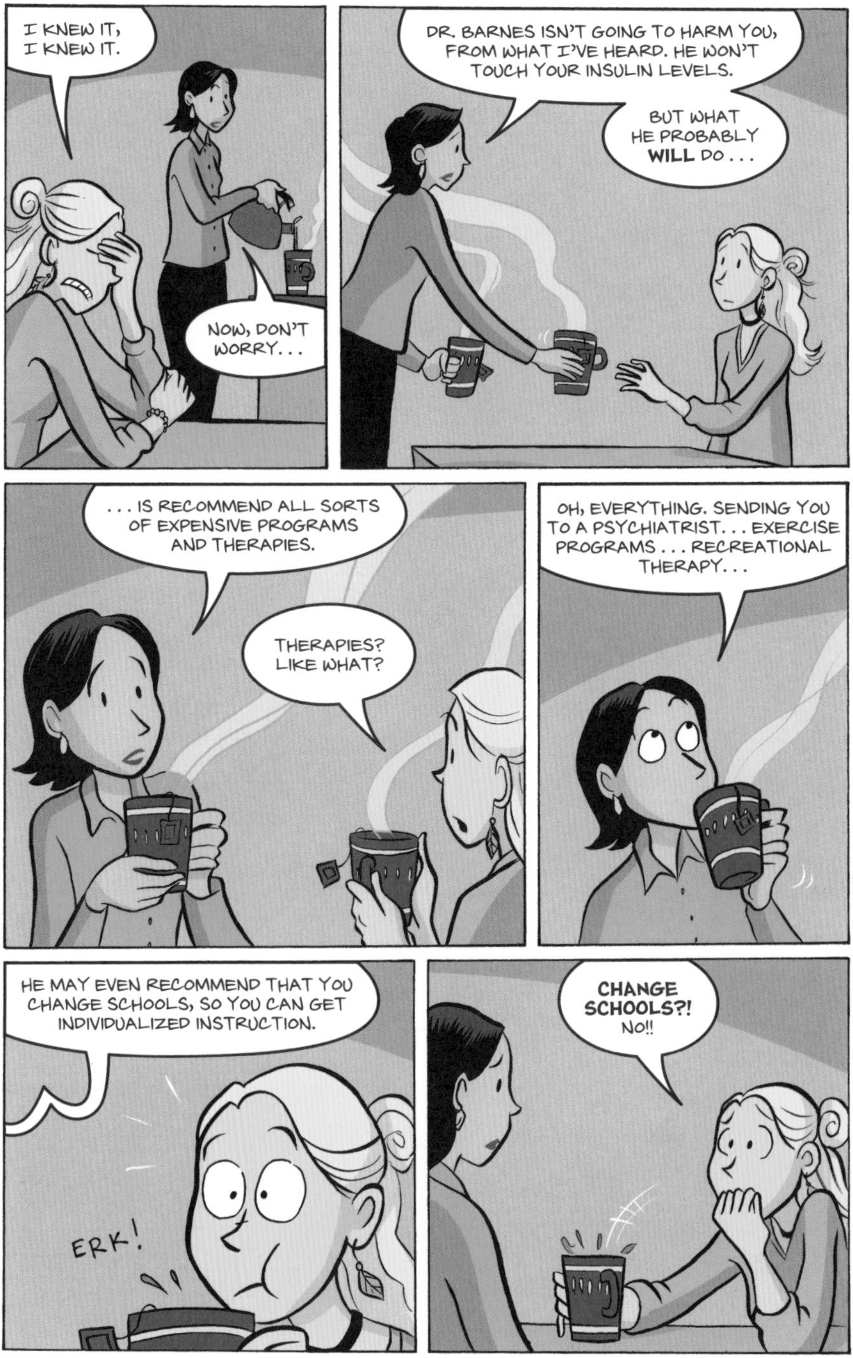

I KNEW IT, I KNEW IT.
NOW, DON'T WORRY...
DR. BARNES ISN'T GOING TO HARM YOU, FROM WHAT I'VE HEARD. HE WON'T TOUCH YOUR INSULIN LEVELS.
BUT WHAT HE PROBABLY **WILL** DO...
...IS RECOMMEND ALL SORTS OF EXPENSIVE PROGRAMS AND THERAPIES.
THERAPIES? LIKE WHAT?
OH, EVERYTHING. SENDING YOU TO A PSYCHIATRIST... EXERCISE PROGRAMS... RECREATIONAL THERAPY...
HE MAY EVEN RECOMMEND THAT YOU CHANGE SCHOOLS, SO YOU CAN GET INDIVIDUALIZED INSTRUCTION.
ERK!
CHANGE SCHOOLS?! NO!!

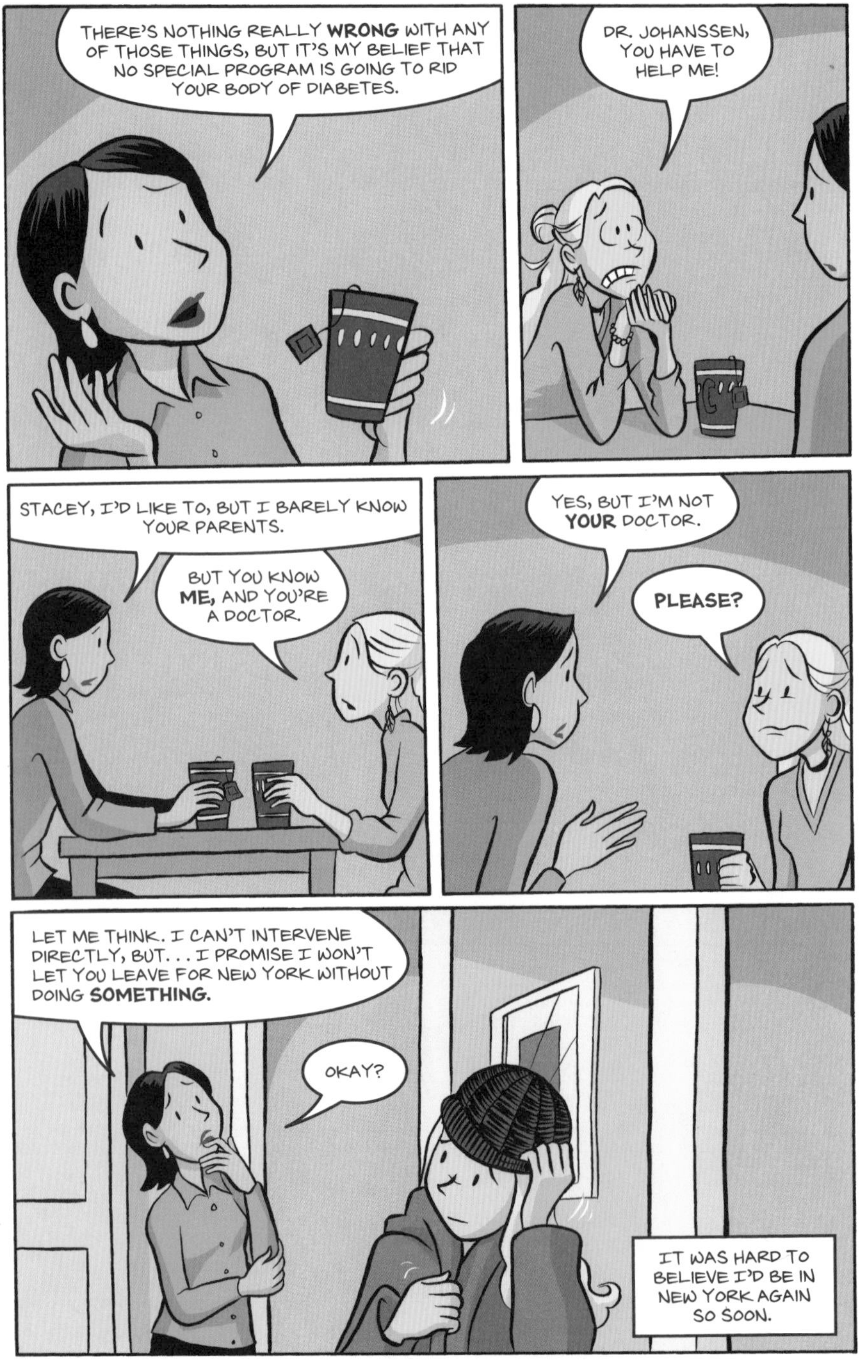
THERE'S NOTHING REALLY WRONG WITH ANY OF THOSE THINGS, BUT IT'S MY BELIEF THAT NO SPECIAL PROGRAM IS GOING TO RID YOUR BODY OF DIABETES.
DR. JOHANSSEN, YOU HAVE TO HELP ME!
STACEY, I'D LIKE TO, BUT I BARELY KNOW YOUR PARENTS.
BUT YOU KNOW ME, AND YOU'RE A DOCTOR.
YES, BUT I'M NOT YOUR DOCTOR.
PLEASE?
LET ME THINK. I CAN'T INTERVENE DIRECTLY, BUT. . . I PROMISE I WON'T LET YOU LEAVE FOR NEW YORK WITHOUT DOING SOMETHING.
OKAY?
IT WAS HARD TO BELIEVE I'D BE IN NEW YORK AGAIN SO SOON.

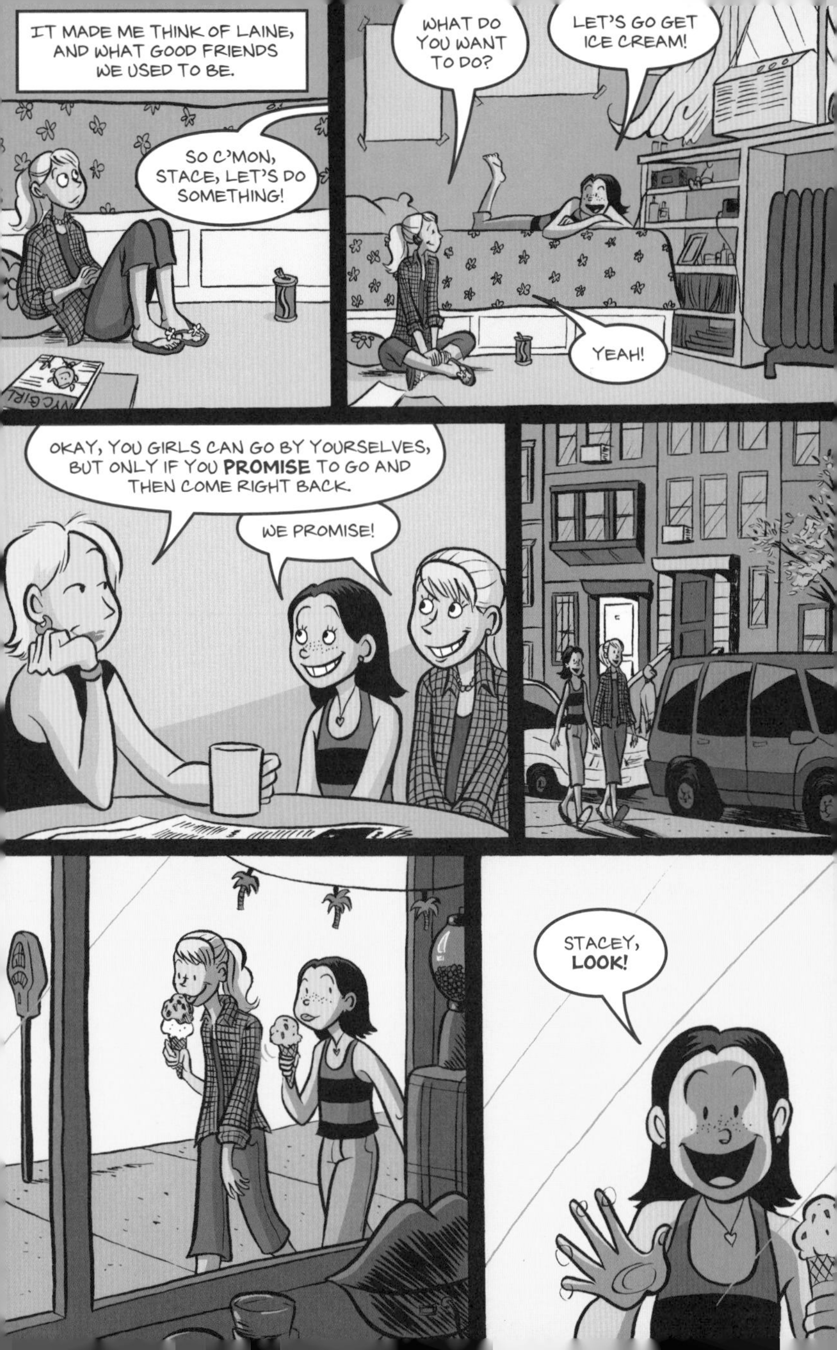
IT MADE ME THINK OF LAINE, AND WHAT GOOD FRIENDS WE USED TO BE.
SO C'MON, STACE, LET'S DO SOMETHING!
WHAT DO YOU WANT TO DO?
LET'S GO GET ICE CREAM!
YEAH!
NYC GIRL
OKAY, YOU GIRLS CAN GO BY YOURSELVES, BUT ONLY IF YOU **PROMISE** TO GO AND THEN COME RIGHT BACK.
WE PROMISE!
STACEY, **LOOK!**

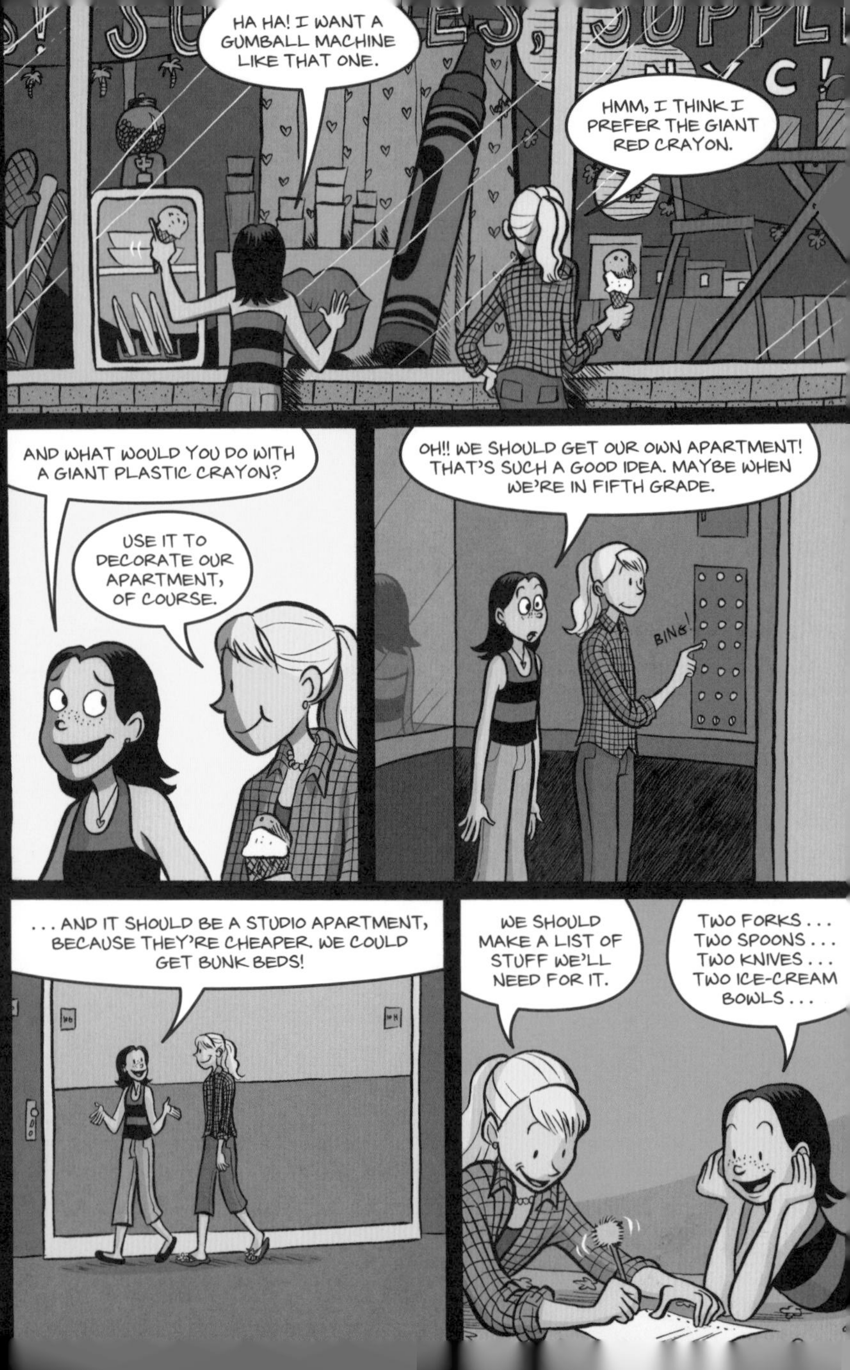
HA HA! I WANT A GUMBALL MACHINE LIKE THAT ONE.
HMM, I THINK I PREFER THE GIANT RED CRAYON.
AND WHAT WOULD YOU DO WITH A GIANT PLASTIC CRAYON?
USE IT TO DECORATE OUR APARTMENT, OF COURSE.
OH!! WE SHOULD GET OUR OWN APARTMENT! THAT'S SUCH A GOOD IDEA. MAYBE WHEN WE'RE IN FIFTH GRADE.
BING!
. . . AND IT SHOULD BE A STUDIO APARTMENT, BECAUSE THEY'RE CHEAPER. WE COULD GET BUNK BEDS!
WE SHOULD MAKE A LIST OF STUFF WE'LL NEED FOR IT.
TWO FORKS . . . TWO SPOONS . . . TWO KNIVES . . . TWO ICE-CREAM BOWLS . . .

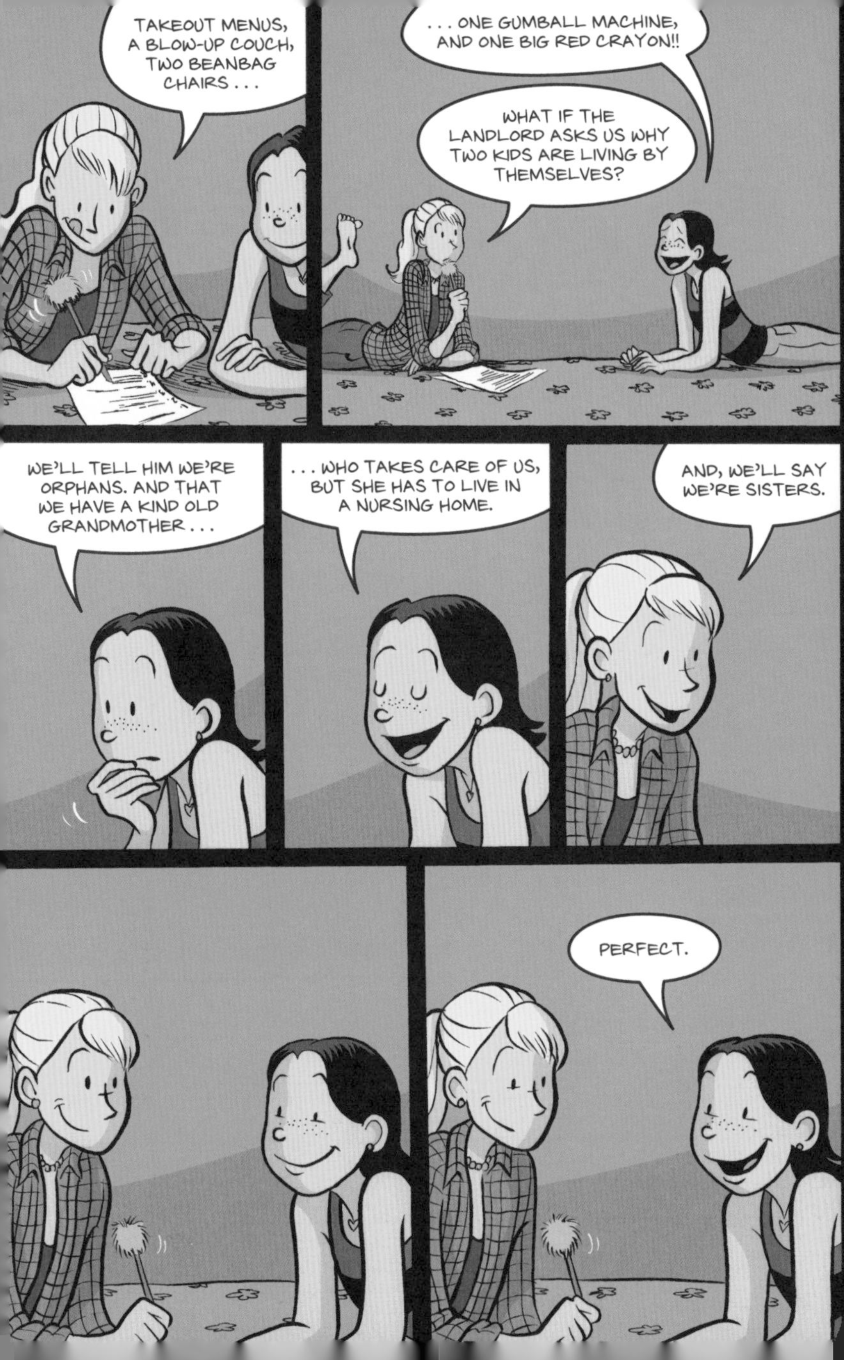
TAKEOUT MENUS, A BLOW-UP COUCH, TWO BEANBAG CHAIRS . . .
. . . ONE GUMBALL MACHINE, AND ONE BIG RED CRAYON!!
WHAT IF THE LANDLORD ASKS US WHY TWO KIDS ARE LIVING BY THEMSELVES?
WE'LL TELL HIM WE'RE ORPHANS. AND THAT WE HAVE A KIND OLD GRANDMOTHER . . .
. . . WHO TAKES CARE OF US, BUT SHE HAS TO LIVE IN A NURSING HOME.
AND, WE'LL SAY WE'RE SISTERS.
PERFECT.

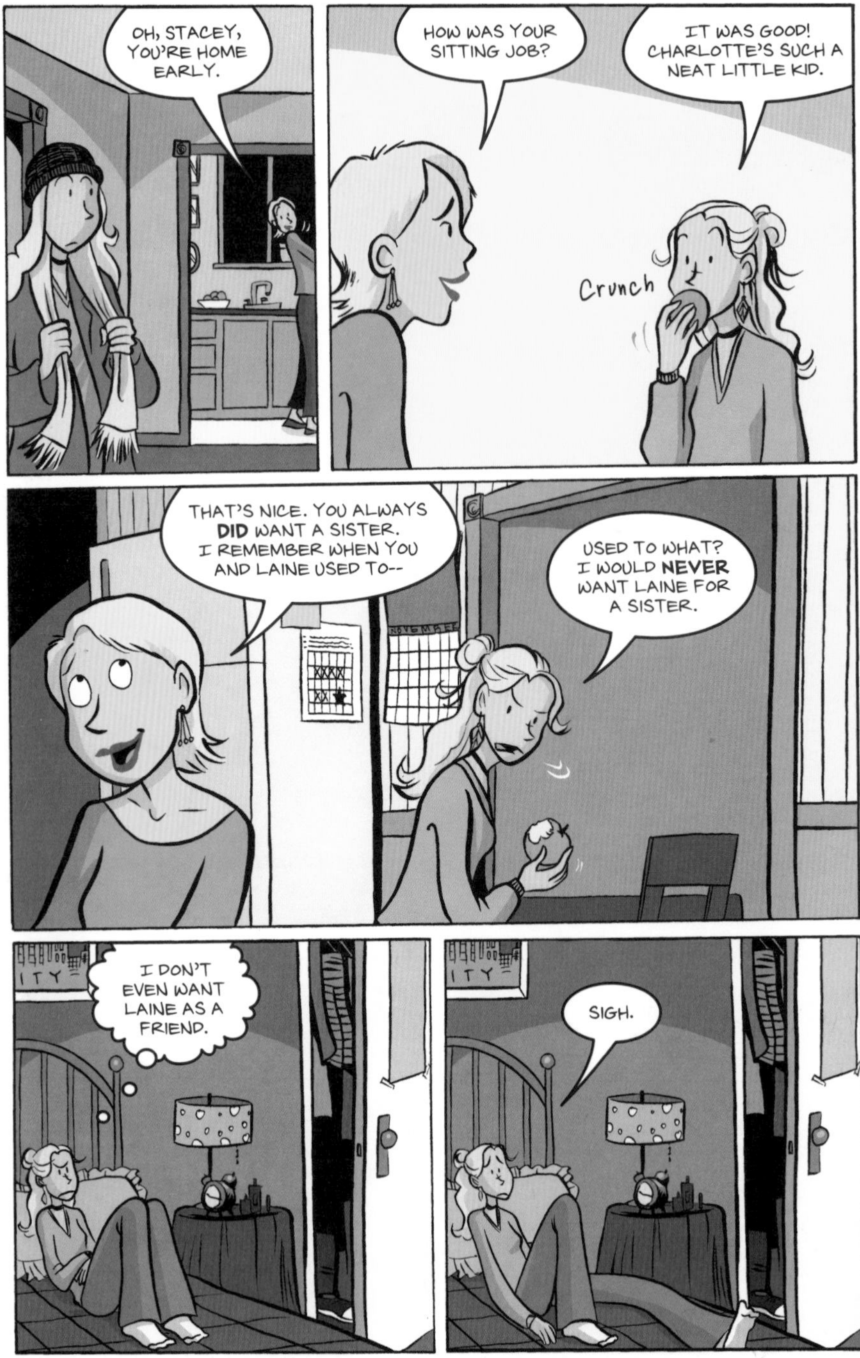
OH, STACEY, YOU'RE HOME EARLY.
HOW WAS YOUR SITTING JOB?
IT WAS GOOD! CHARLOTTE'S SUCH A NEAT LITTLE KID.
Crunch
THAT'S NICE. YOU ALWAYS **DID** WANT A SISTER. I REMEMBER WHEN YOU AND LAINE USED TO--
USED TO WHAT? I WOULD **NEVER** WANT LAINE FOR A SISTER.
I DON'T EVEN WANT LAINE AS A FRIEND.
SIGH.

CHAPTER 8

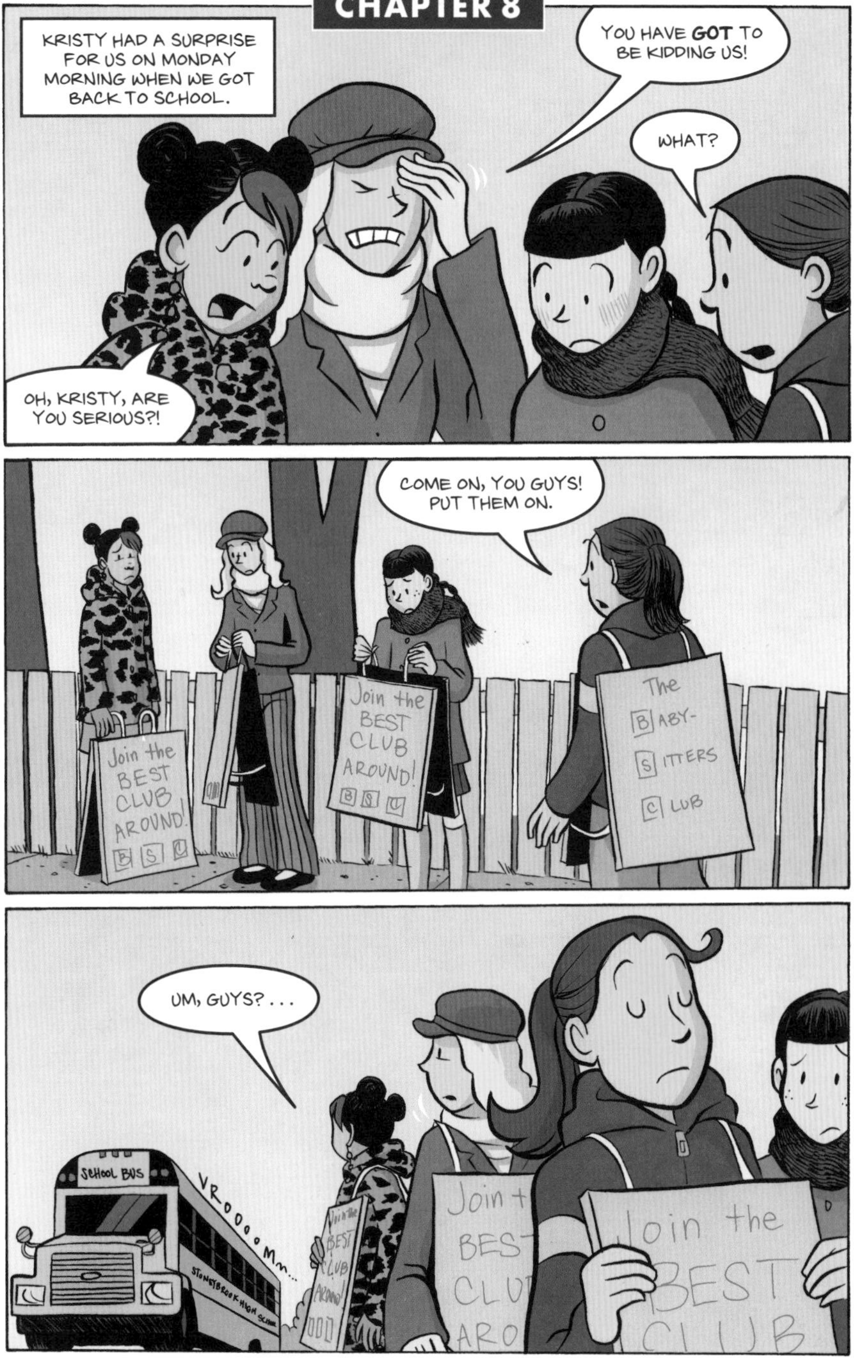
KRISTY HAD A SURPRISE FOR US ON MONDAY MORNING WHEN WE GOT BACK TO SCHOOL.
YOU HAVE **GOT** TO BE KIDDING US!
WHAT?
OH, KRISTY, ARE YOU SERIOUS?!
COME ON, YOU GUYS! PUT THEM ON.
Join the BEST CLUB AROUND! BSC
Join the BEST CLUB AROUND! BSC
The BABY-SITTERS CLUB
UM, GUYS? . . .
SCHOOL BUS
VROooomm...
Join the BEST CLUB AROUND
Join the BEST CLUB

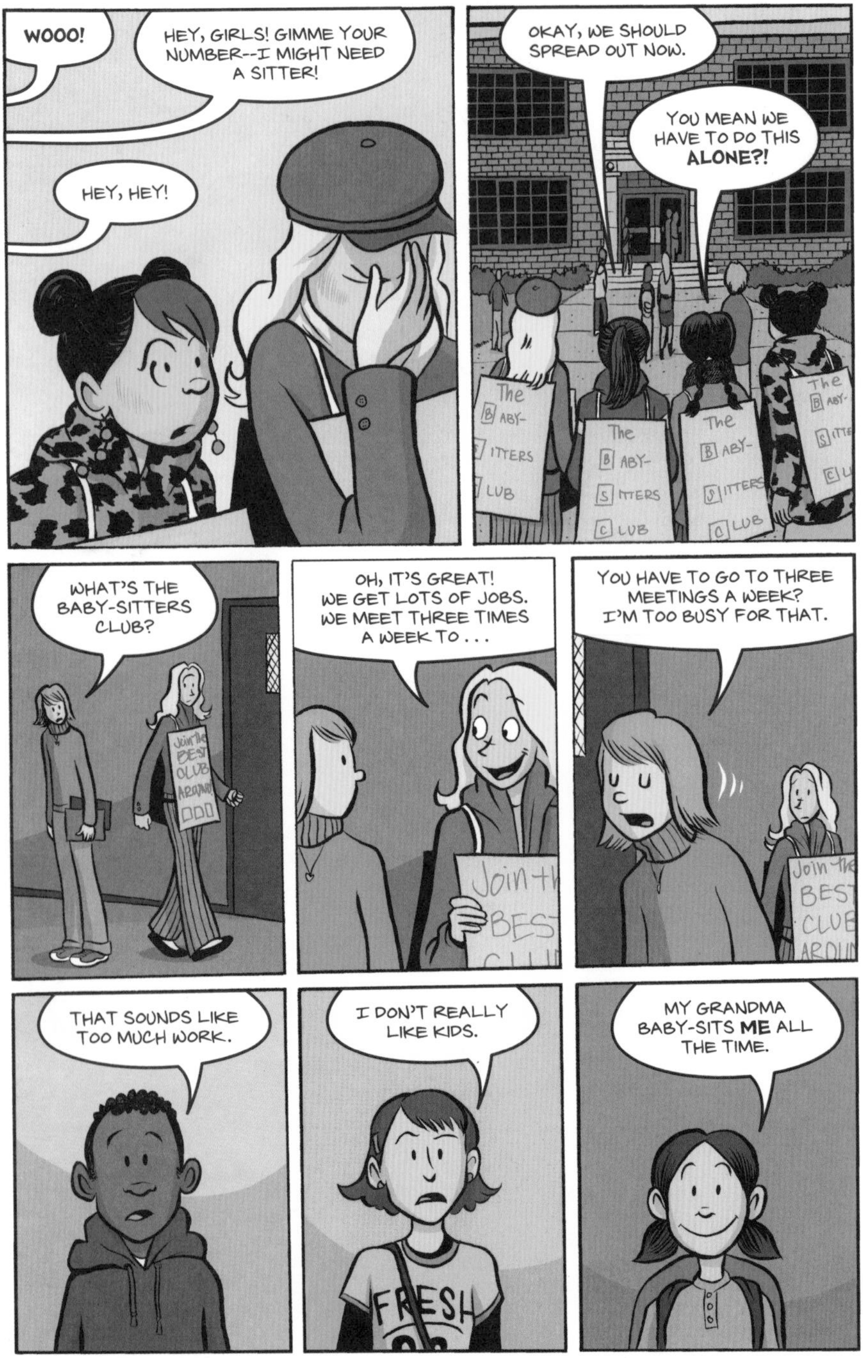
WOOO!
HEY, GIRLS! GIMME YOUR NUMBER--I MIGHT NEED A SITTER!
HEY, HEY!
OKAY, WE SHOULD SPREAD OUT NOW.
YOU MEAN WE HAVE TO DO THIS **ALONE?!**
The B ABY- S ITTERS C LUB
WHAT'S THE BABY-SITTERS CLUB?
OH, IT'S GREAT! WE GET LOTS OF JOBS. WE MEET THREE TIMES A WEEK TO . . .
YOU HAVE TO GO TO THREE MEETINGS A WEEK? I'M TOO BUSY FOR THAT.
THAT SOUNDS LIKE TOO MUCH WORK.
I DON'T REALLY LIKE KIDS.
FRESH
MY GRANDMA BABY-SITS **ME** ALL THE TIME.

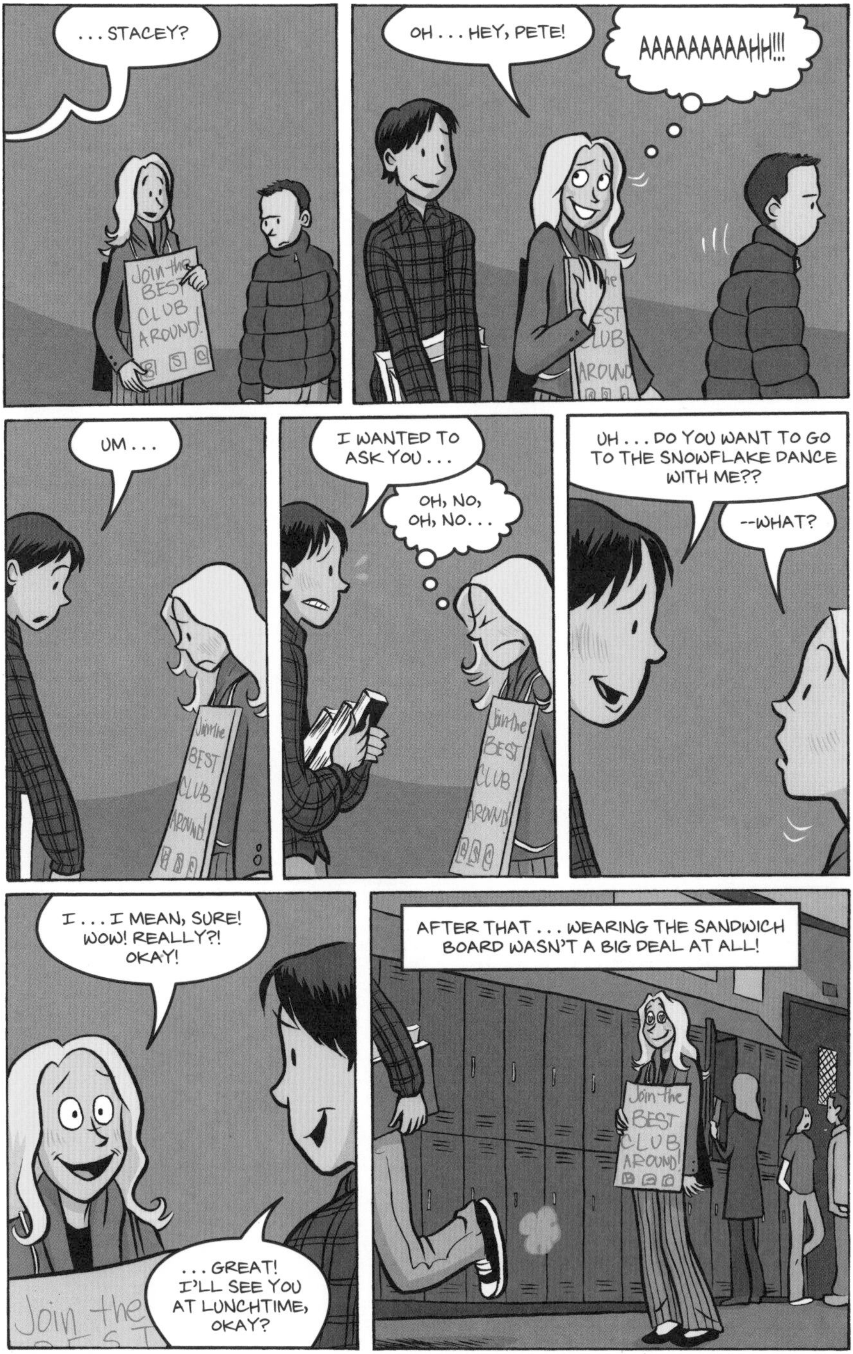
. . . STACEY?
OH . . . HEY, PETE!
AAAAAAAAAAHH!!!
Join the BEST CLUB AROUND!
UM . . .
I WANTED TO ASK YOU . . .
OH, NO, OH, NO . . .
UH . . . DO YOU WANT TO GO TO THE SNOWFLAKE DANCE WITH ME??
--WHAT?
I . . . I MEAN, SURE! WOW! REALLY?! OKAY!
. . . GREAT! I'LL SEE YOU AT LUNCHTIME, OKAY?
AFTER THAT . . . WEARING THE SANDWICH BOARD WASN'T A BIG DEAL AT ALL!

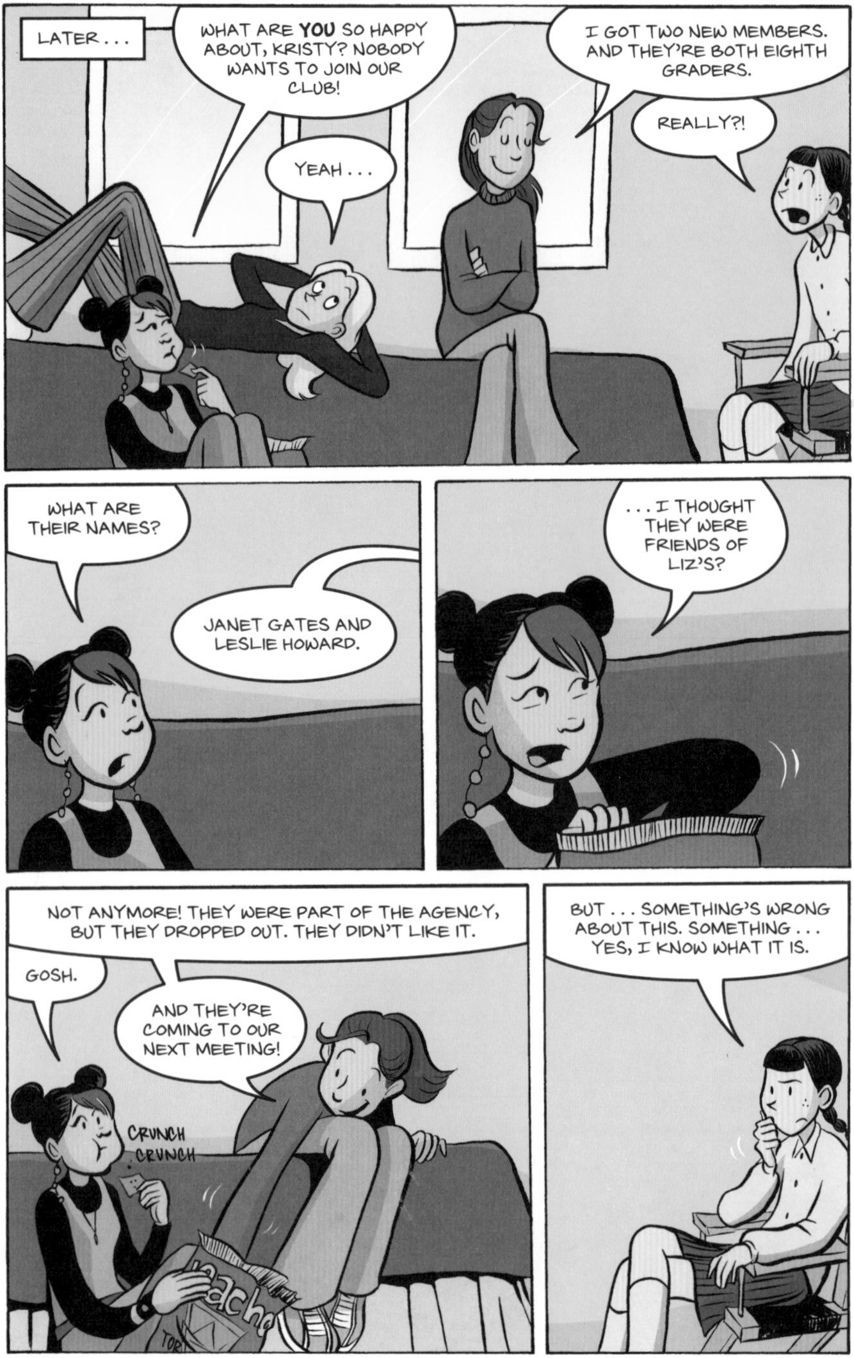
LATER . . .
WHAT ARE **YOU** SO HAPPY ABOUT, KRISTY? NOBODY WANTS TO JOIN OUR CLUB!
YEAH . . .
I GOT TWO NEW MEMBERS. AND THEY'RE BOTH EIGHTH GRADERS.
REALLY?!
WHAT ARE THEIR NAMES?
JANET GATES AND LESLIE HOWARD.
. . . I THOUGHT THEY WERE FRIENDS OF LIZ'S?
NOT ANYMORE! THEY WERE PART OF THE AGENCY, BUT THEY DROPPED OUT. THEY DIDN'T LIKE IT.
GOSH.
AND THEY'RE COMING TO OUR NEXT MEETING!
CRUNCH
CRUNCH
BUT . . . SOMETHING'S WRONG ABOUT THIS. SOMETHING . . . YES, I KNOW WHAT IT IS.

69

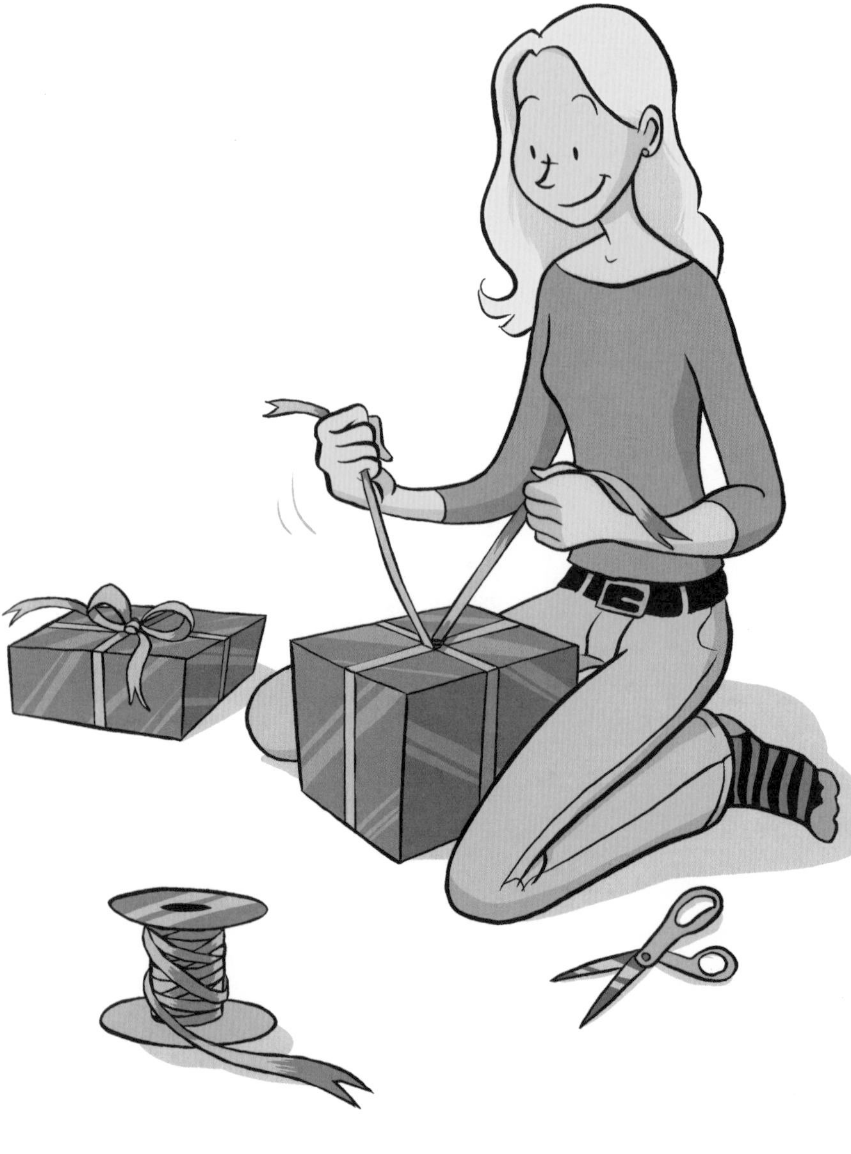

71

74

75

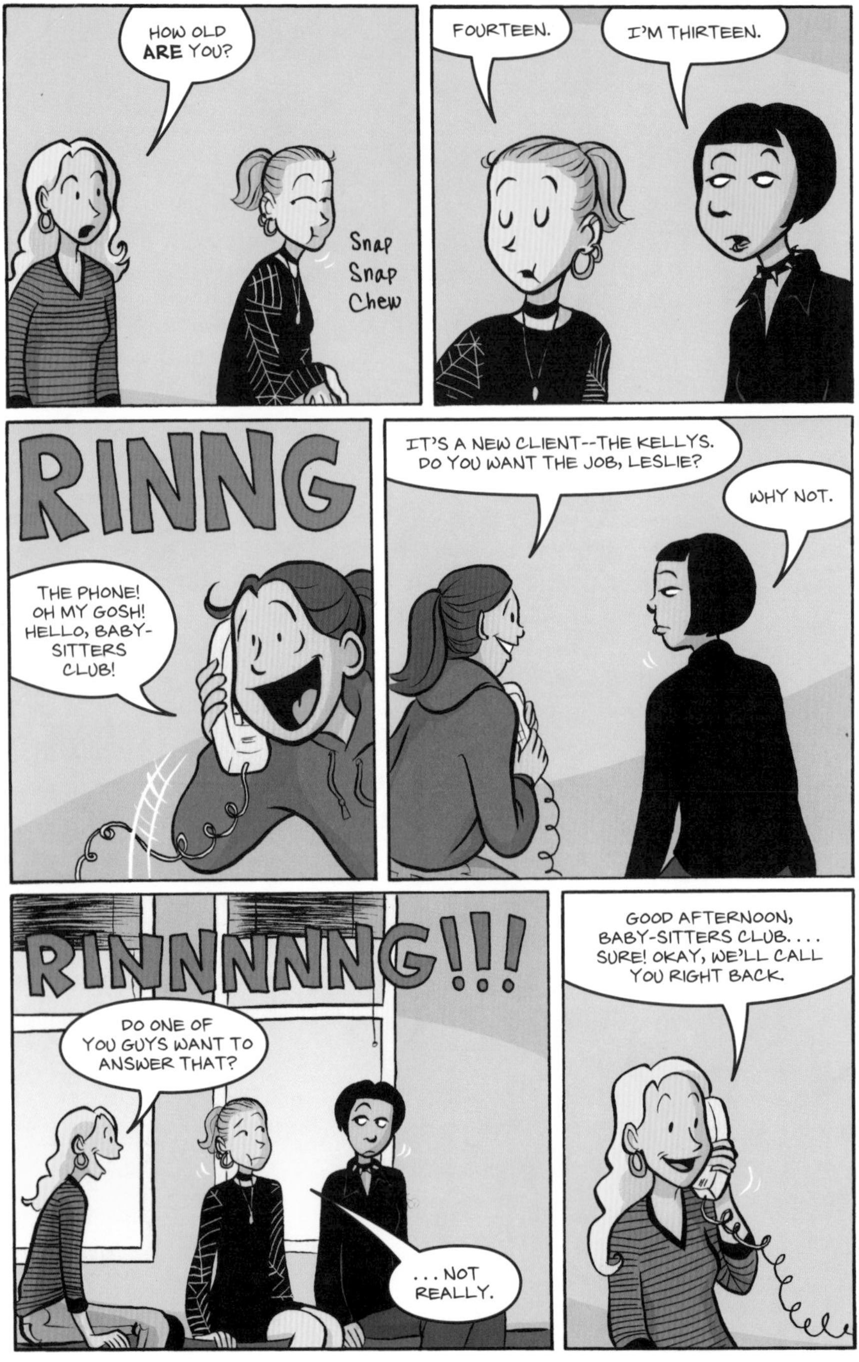
HOW OLD ARE YOU?
Snap Snap Chew
FOURTEEN.
I'M THIRTEEN.
RINNG
THE PHONE! OH MY GOSH! HELLO, BABY-SITTERS CLUB!
IT'S A NEW CLIENT--THE KELLYS. DO YOU WANT THE JOB, LESLIE?
WHY NOT.
RINNNNNG!!!
DO ONE OF YOU GUYS WANT TO ANSWER THAT?
. . . NOT REALLY.
GOOD AFTERNOON, BABY-SITTERS CLUB. . . . SURE! OKAY, WE'LL CALL YOU RIGHT BACK.

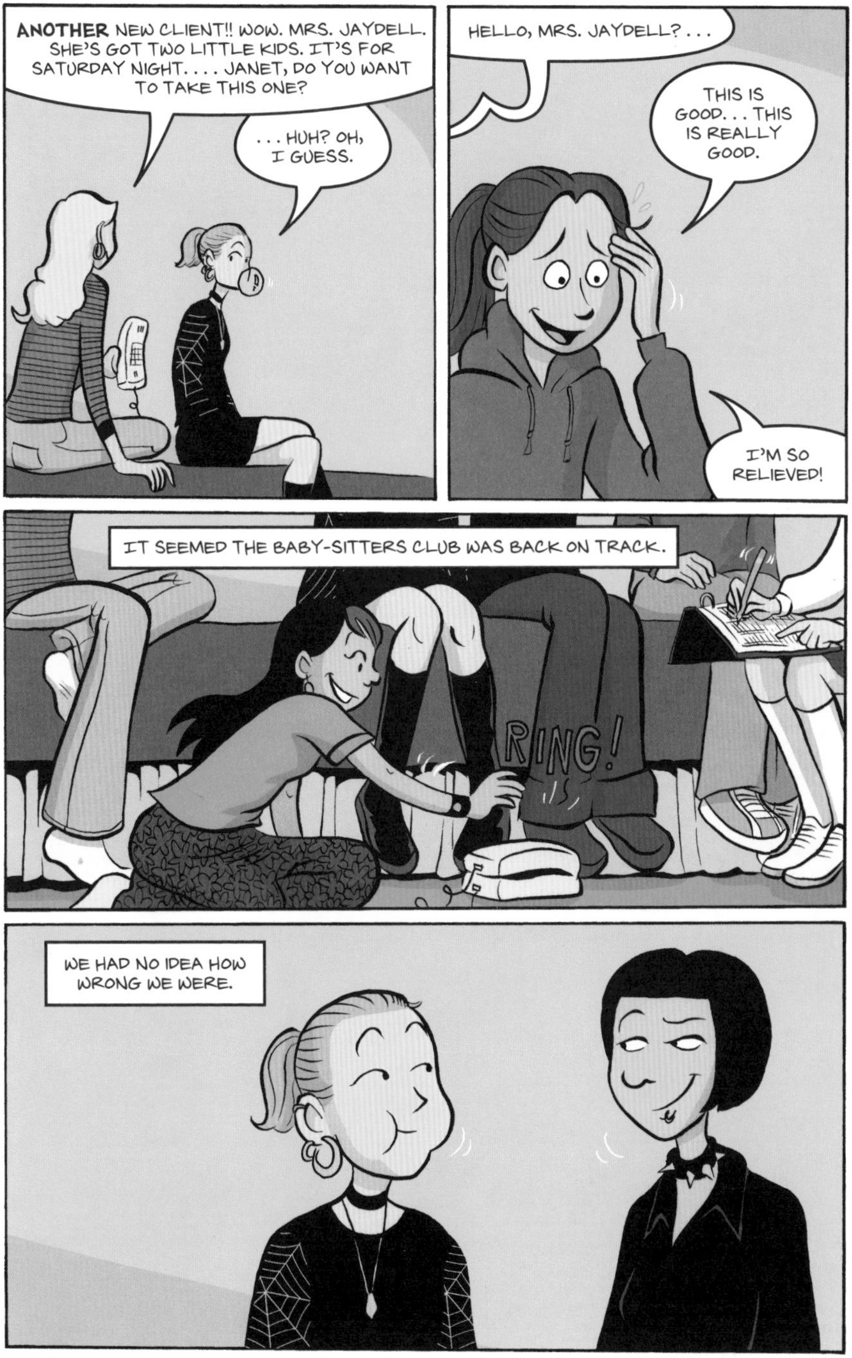
ANOTHER NEW CLIENT!! WOW. MRS. JAYDELL. SHE'S GOT TWO LITTLE KIDS. IT'S FOR SATURDAY NIGHT. . . . JANET, DO YOU WANT TO TAKE THIS ONE?
. . . HUH? OH, I GUESS.
HELLO, MRS. JAYDELL? . . .
THIS IS GOOD. . . THIS IS REALLY GOOD.
I'M SO RELIEVED!
IT SEEMED THE BABY-SITTERS CLUB WAS BACK ON TRACK.
RING!
WE HAD NO IDEA HOW WRONG WE WERE.

Monday, December 8

Today Kristy, Stacey + Mary Anne all
arived early for our baby-sitters club
meeting. We were all realy excited to find
out how Janet and Leslie's siting jobs
had gone on ~~Sto~~ Saturday.

  When it was 5:30 we kept expecting the
doorbell to ring any seconde. But it
didnt. Soon it was 5:50. Where were
they. Krist was getting worried. ~~Wret~~ Write
this down in our notebook, somebody,
she said. Somethings wrong.

                              * Claudia *

85

Wednesday, December 10th

Earlier this afternoon, I baby-sat for Jamie
while Mrs. Newton took Lucy to a doctor's
appointment. Something was bothering him. He
moped around as if he'd lost his best friend.
He greeted me cheerfully enough when I
arrived, but as soon as Mrs. Newton carried
a bundled-up Lucy out the back door, his
face fell....

                    Mary Anne

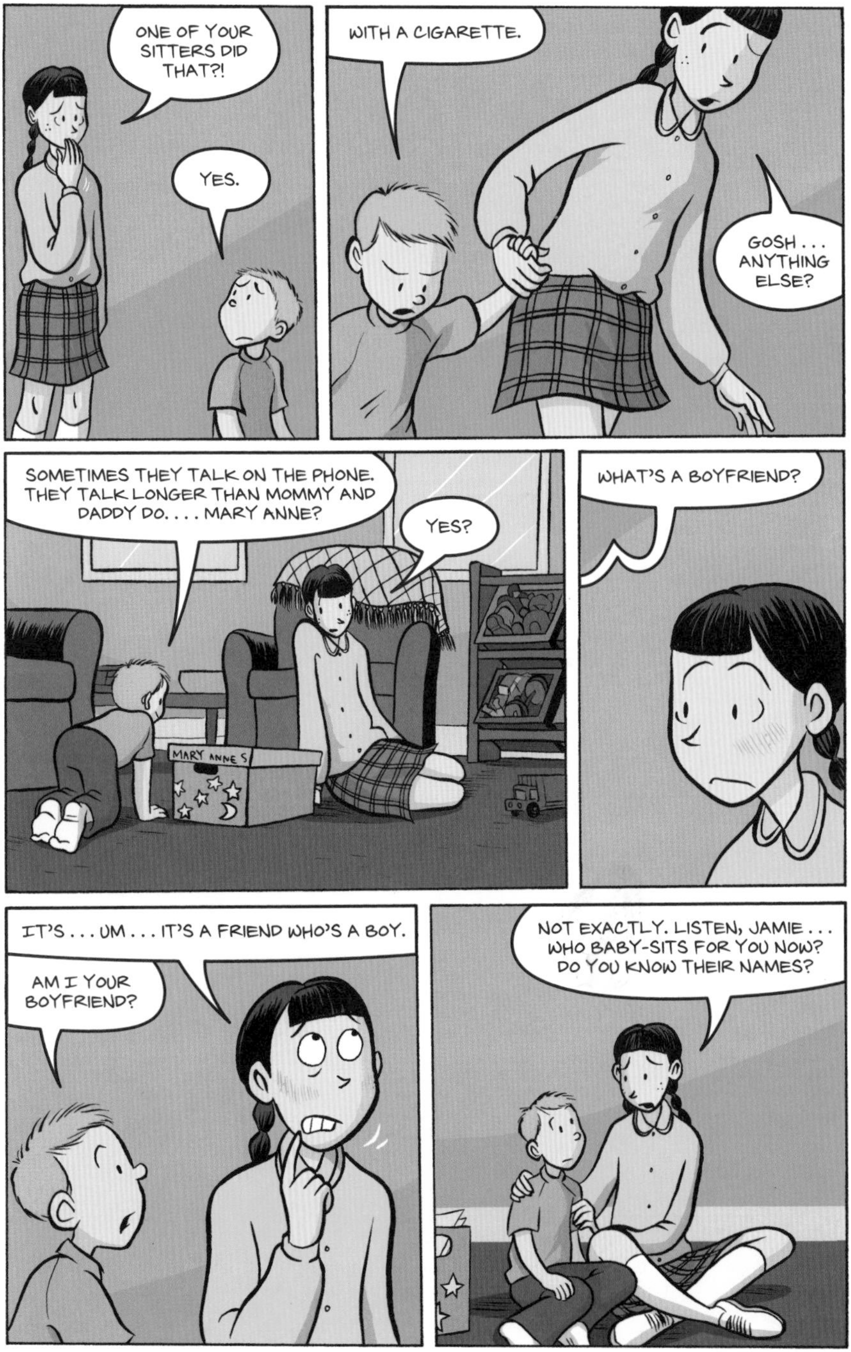

ONE OF YOUR SITTERS DID THAT?!
YES.
WITH A CIGARETTE.
GOSH . . . ANYTHING ELSE?
SOMETIMES THEY TALK ON THE PHONE. THEY TALK LONGER THAN MOMMY AND DADDY DO. . . . MARY ANNE?
YES?
MARY ANNE'S
WHAT'S A BOYFRIEND?
IT'S . . . UM . . . IT'S A FRIEND WHO'S A BOY.
AM I YOUR BOYFRIEND?
NOT EXACTLY. LISTEN, JAMIE . . . WHO BABY-SITS FOR YOU NOW? DO YOU KNOW THEIR NAMES?

93

94

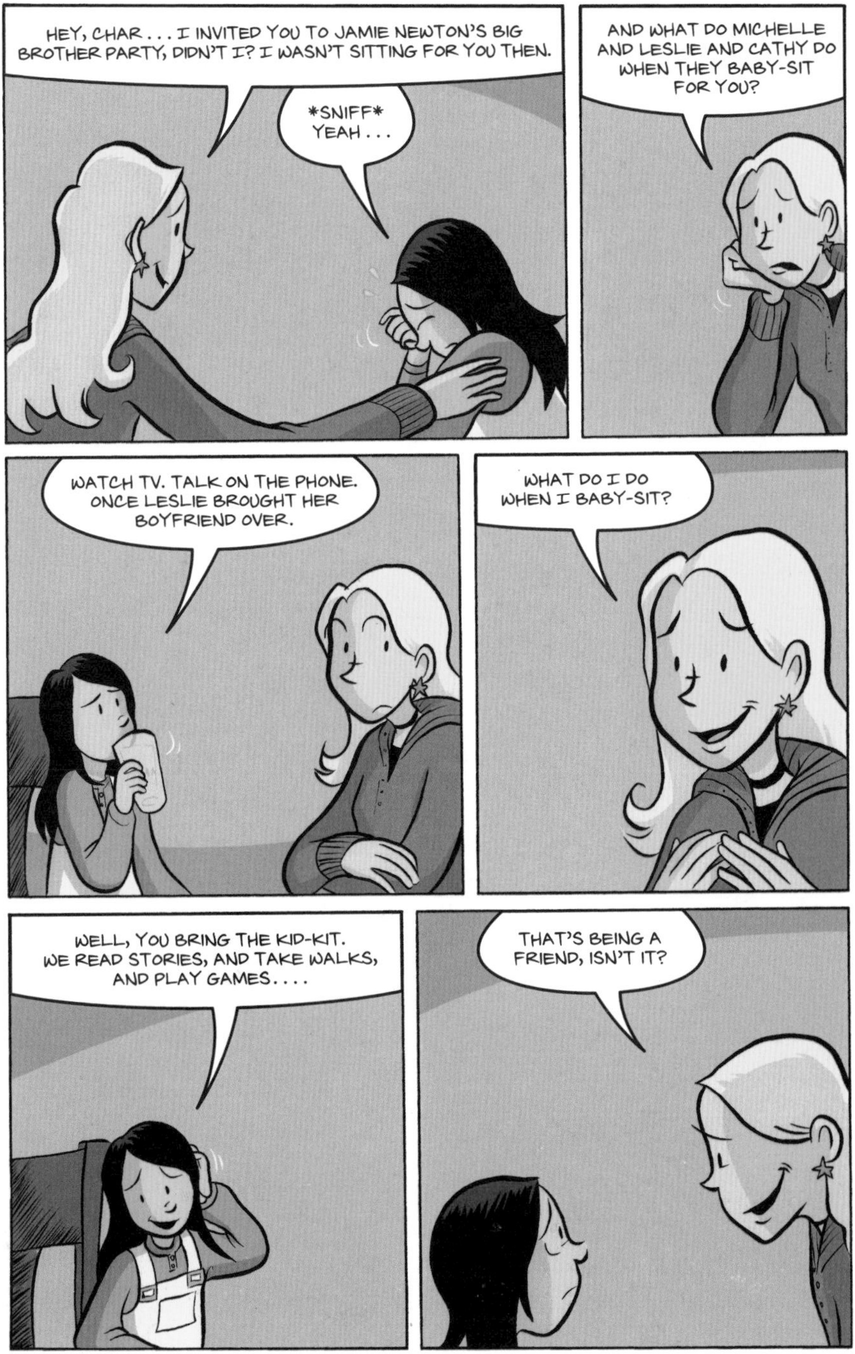
HEY, CHAR . . . I INVITED YOU TO JAMIE NEWTON'S BIG BROTHER PARTY, DIDN'T I? I WASN'T SITTING FOR YOU THEN.
SNIFF YEAH . . .
AND WHAT DO MICHELLE AND LESLIE AND CATHY DO WHEN THEY BABY-SIT FOR YOU?
WATCH TV. TALK ON THE PHONE. ONCE LESLIE BROUGHT HER BOYFRIEND OVER.
WHAT DO I DO WHEN I BABY-SIT?
WELL, YOU BRING THE KID-KIT. WE READ STORIES, AND TAKE WALKS, AND PLAY GAMES. . . .
THAT'S BEING A FRIEND, ISN'T IT?

96

100

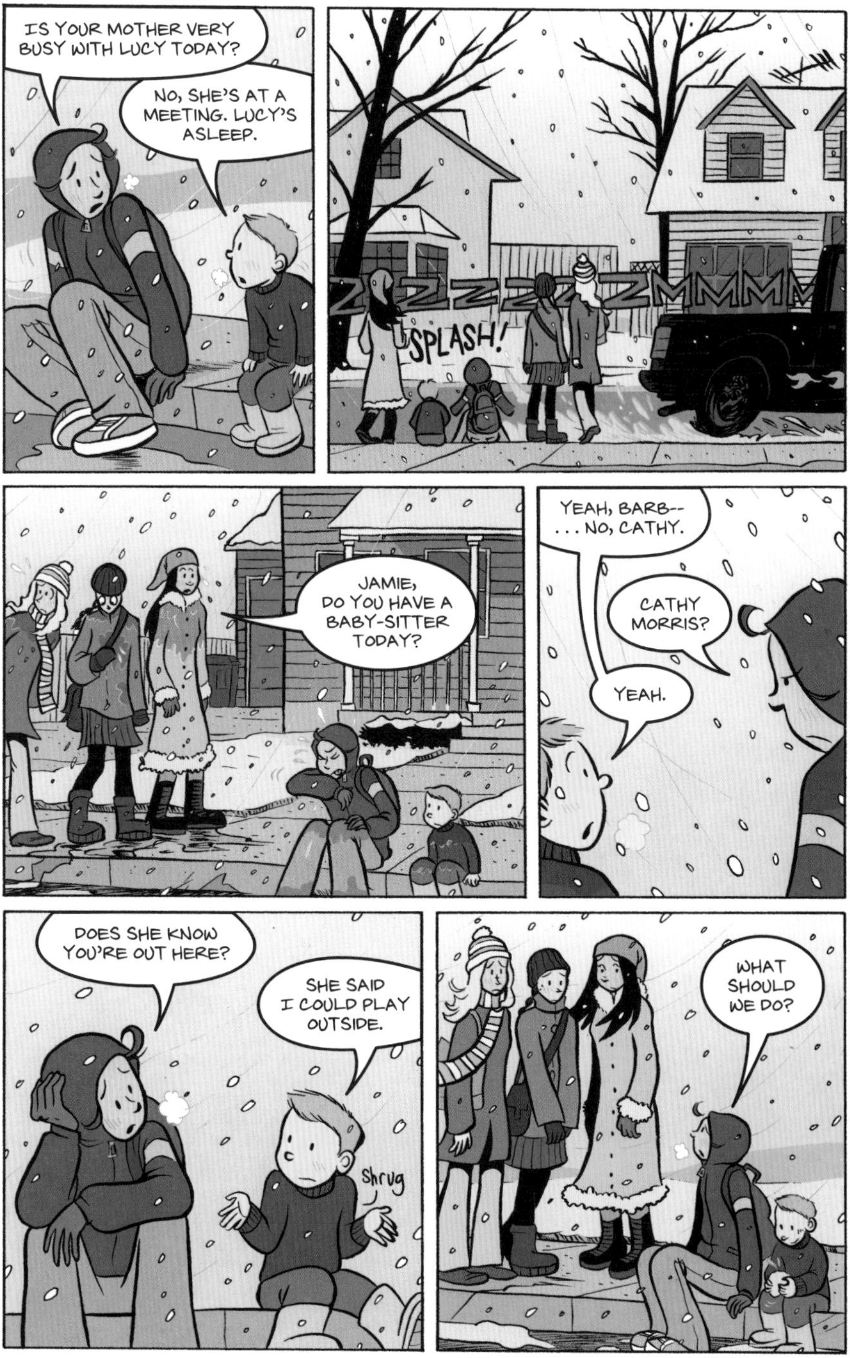
IS YOUR MOTHER VERY BUSY WITH LUCY TODAY?
NO, SHE'S AT A MEETING. LUCY'S ASLEEP.
ZZZZZZZMMMMM
SPLASH!
JAMIE, DO YOU HAVE A BABY-SITTER TODAY?
YEAH, BARB-- . . . NO, CATHY.
CATHY MORRIS?
YEAH.
DOES SHE KNOW YOU'RE OUT HERE?
SHE SAID I COULD PLAY OUTSIDE.
shrug
WHAT SHOULD WE DO?

103

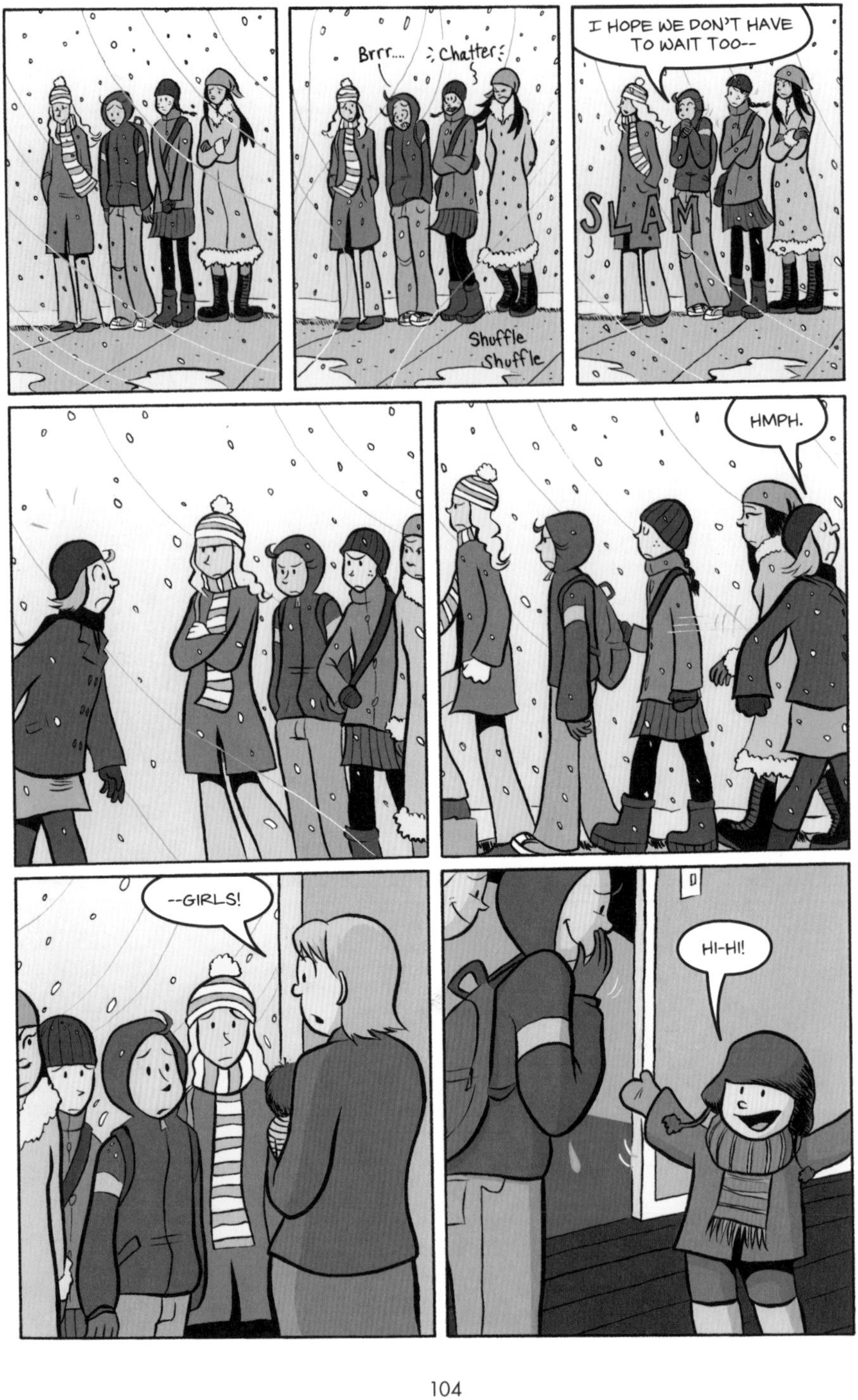
Brrr....
Chatter
I HOPE WE DON'T HAVE TO WAIT TOO--
SLAM
Shuffle Shuffle
HMPH.
--GIRLS!
HI-HI!

105

107

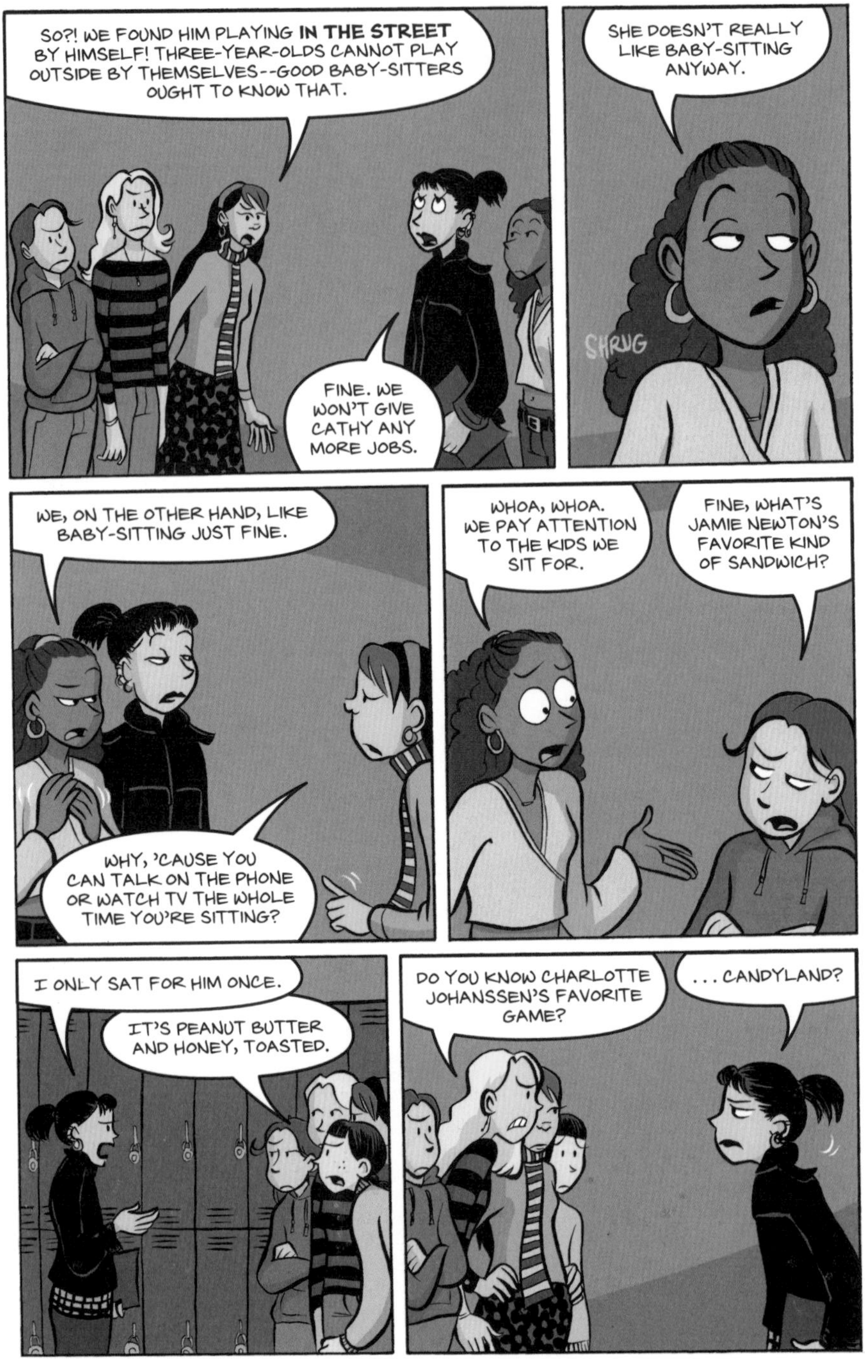
SO?! WE FOUND HIM PLAYING IN THE STREET BY HIMSELF! THREE-YEAR-OLDS CANNOT PLAY OUTSIDE BY THEMSELVES--GOOD BABY-SITTERS OUGHT TO KNOW THAT.
FINE. WE WON'T GIVE CATHY ANY MORE JOBS.
SHE DOESN'T REALLY LIKE BABY-SITTING ANYWAY.
SHRUG
WE, ON THE OTHER HAND, LIKE BABY-SITTING JUST FINE.
WHY, 'CAUSE YOU CAN TALK ON THE PHONE OR WATCH TV THE WHOLE TIME YOU'RE SITTING?
WHOA, WHOA. WE PAY ATTENTION TO THE KIDS WE SIT FOR.
FINE, WHAT'S JAMIE NEWTON'S FAVORITE KIND OF SANDWICH?
I ONLY SAT FOR HIM ONCE.
IT'S PEANUT BUTTER AND HONEY, TOASTED.
DO YOU KNOW CHARLOTTE JOHANSSEN'S FAVORITE GAME?
. . . CANDYLAND?

111

113

114

115

118

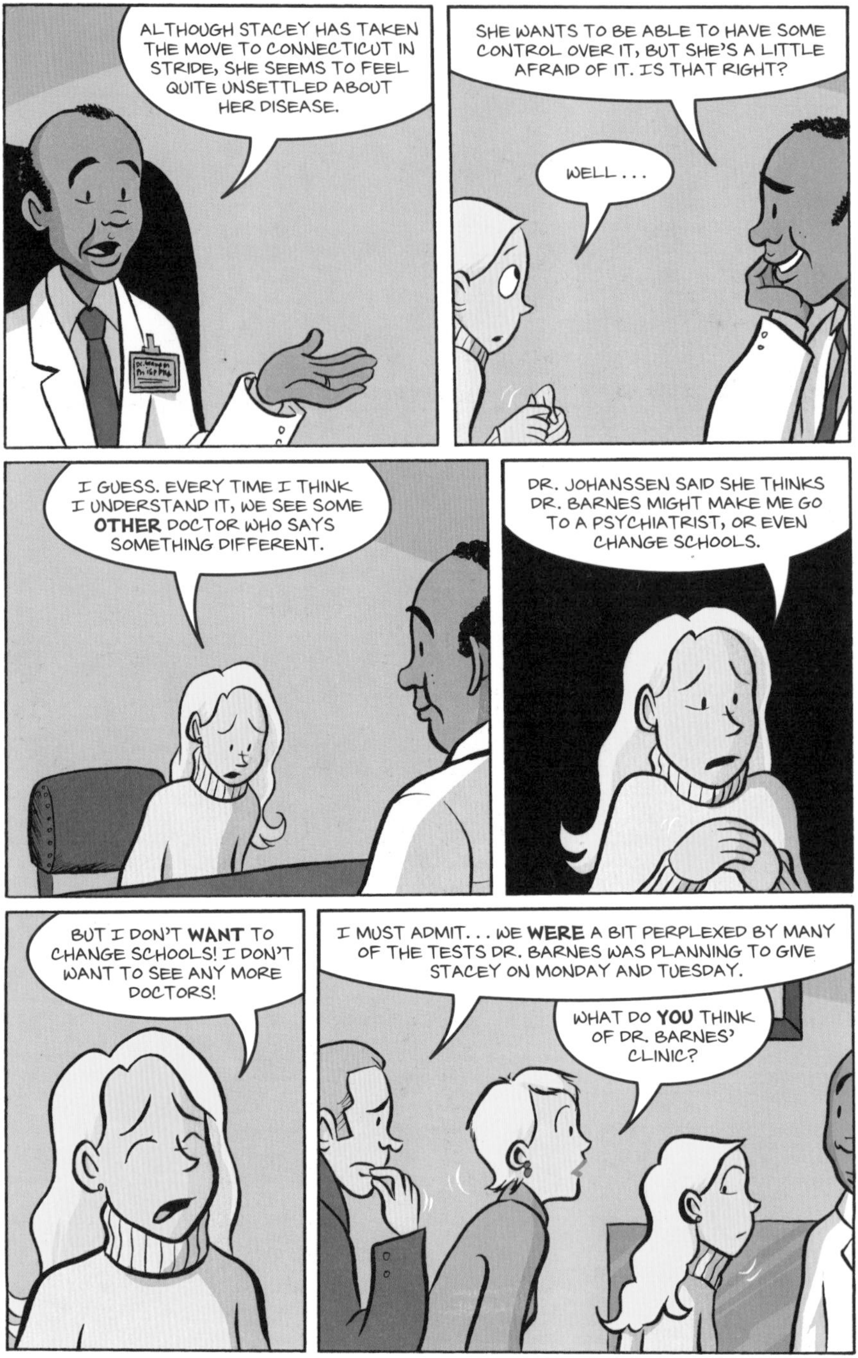

ALTHOUGH STACEY HAS TAKEN THE MOVE TO CONNECTICUT IN STRIDE, SHE SEEMS TO FEEL QUITE UNSETTLED ABOUT HER DISEASE.
SHE WANTS TO BE ABLE TO HAVE SOME CONTROL OVER IT, BUT SHE'S A LITTLE AFRAID OF IT. IS THAT RIGHT?
WELL . . .
I GUESS. EVERY TIME I THINK I UNDERSTAND IT, WE SEE SOME **OTHER** DOCTOR WHO SAYS SOMETHING DIFFERENT.
DR. JOHANSSEN SAID SHE THINKS DR. BARNES MIGHT MAKE ME GO TO A PSYCHIATRIST, OR EVEN CHANGE SCHOOLS.
BUT I DON'T **WANT** TO CHANGE SCHOOLS! I DON'T WANT TO SEE ANY MORE DOCTORS!
I MUST ADMIT. . . WE **WERE** A BIT PERPLEXED BY MANY OF THE TESTS DR. BARNES WAS PLANNING TO GIVE STACEY ON MONDAY AND TUESDAY.
WHAT DO **YOU** THINK OF DR. BARNES' CLINIC?

121

CHAPTER 14

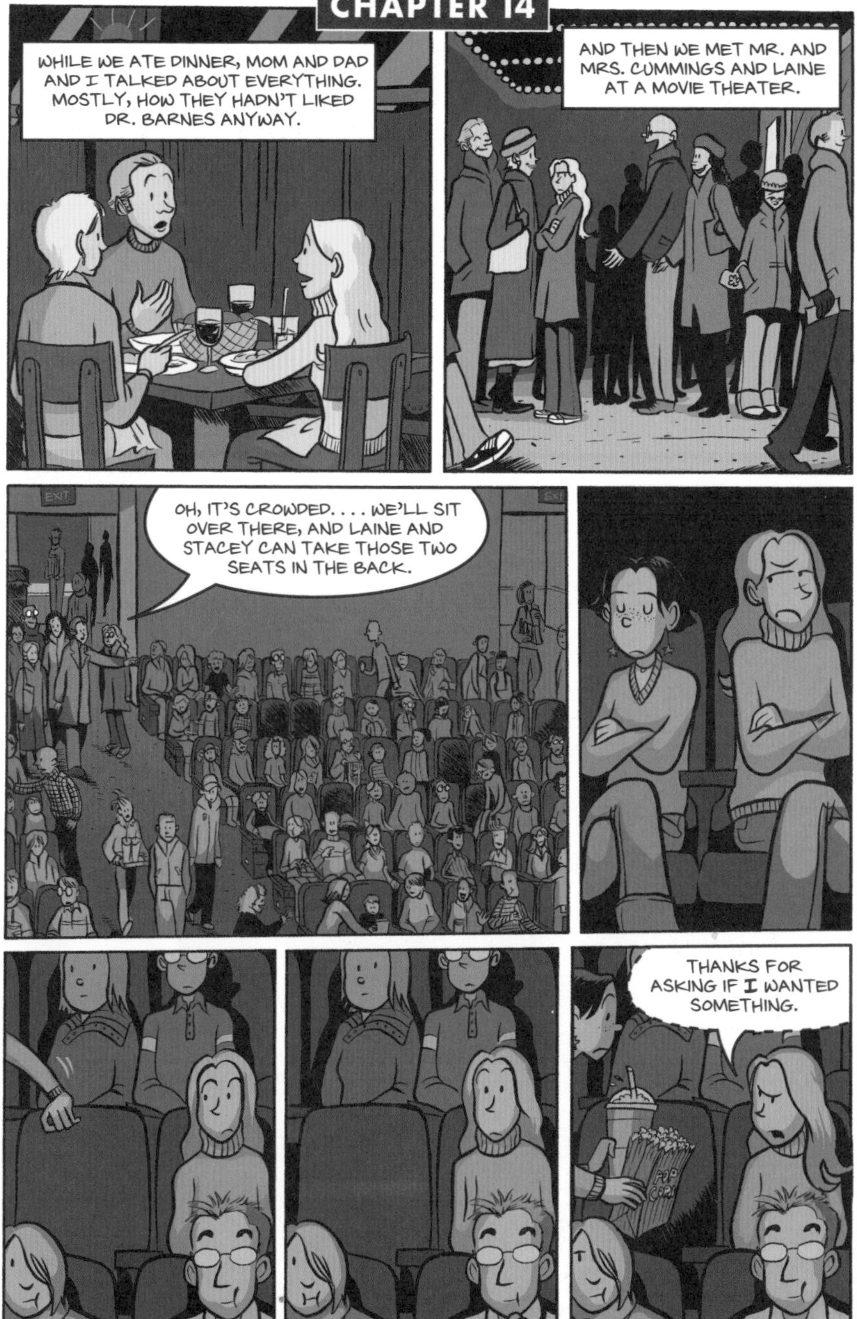
WHILE WE ATE DINNER, MOM AND DAD AND I TALKED ABOUT EVERYTHING. MOSTLY, HOW THEY HADN'T LIKED DR. BARNES ANYWAY.
AND THEN WE MET MR. AND MRS. CUMMINGS AND LAINE AT A MOVIE THEATER.
EXIT
OH, IT'S CROWDED. . . . WE'LL SIT OVER THERE, AND LAINE AND STACEY CAN TAKE THOSE TWO SEATS IN THE BACK.
THANKS FOR ASKING IF I WANTED SOMETHING.

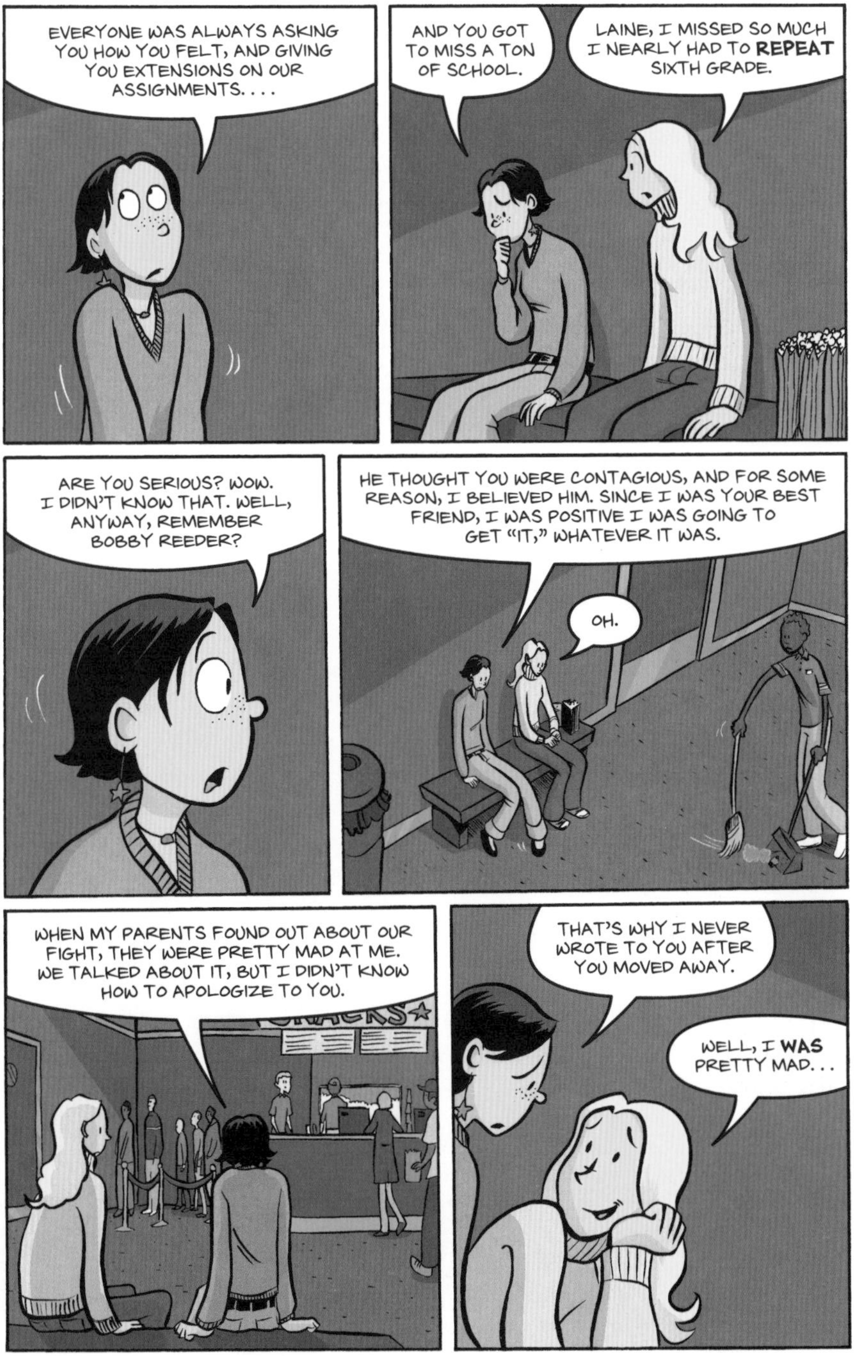
EVERYONE WAS ALWAYS ASKING YOU HOW YOU FELT, AND GIVING YOU EXTENSIONS ON OUR ASSIGNMENTS. . . .
AND YOU GOT TO MISS A TON OF SCHOOL.
LAINE, I MISSED SO MUCH I NEARLY HAD TO **REPEAT** SIXTH GRADE.
ARE YOU SERIOUS? WOW. I DIDN'T KNOW THAT. WELL, ANYWAY, REMEMBER BOBBY REEDER?
HE THOUGHT YOU WERE CONTAGIOUS, AND FOR SOME REASON, I BELIEVED HIM. SINCE I WAS YOUR BEST FRIEND, I WAS POSITIVE I WAS GOING TO GET "IT," WHATEVER IT WAS.
OH.
WHEN MY PARENTS FOUND OUT ABOUT OUR FIGHT, THEY WERE PRETTY MAD AT ME. WE TALKED ABOUT IT, BUT I DIDN'T KNOW HOW TO APOLOGIZE TO YOU.
THAT'S WHY I NEVER WROTE TO YOU AFTER YOU MOVED AWAY.
WELL, I **WAS** PRETTY MAD. . .

128

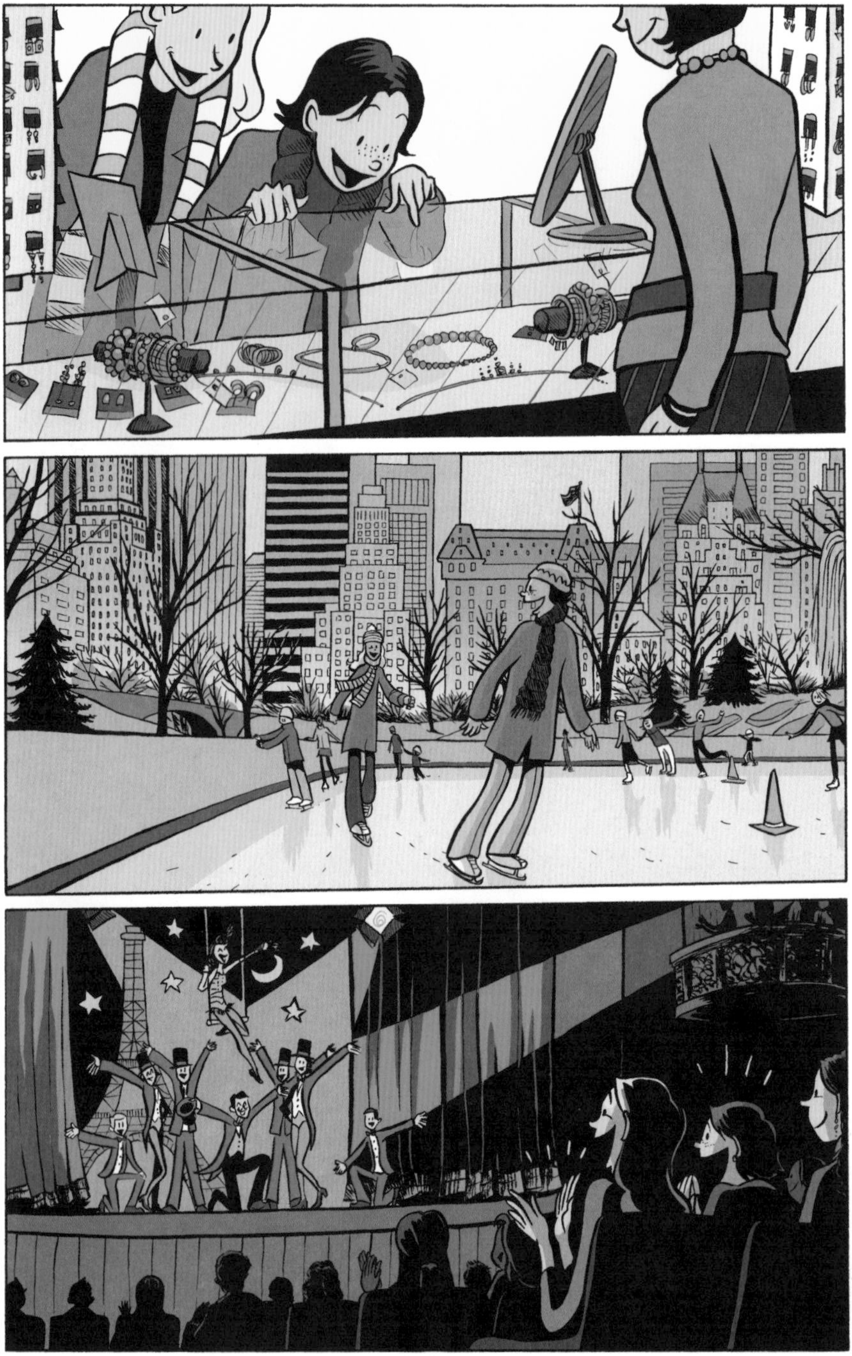

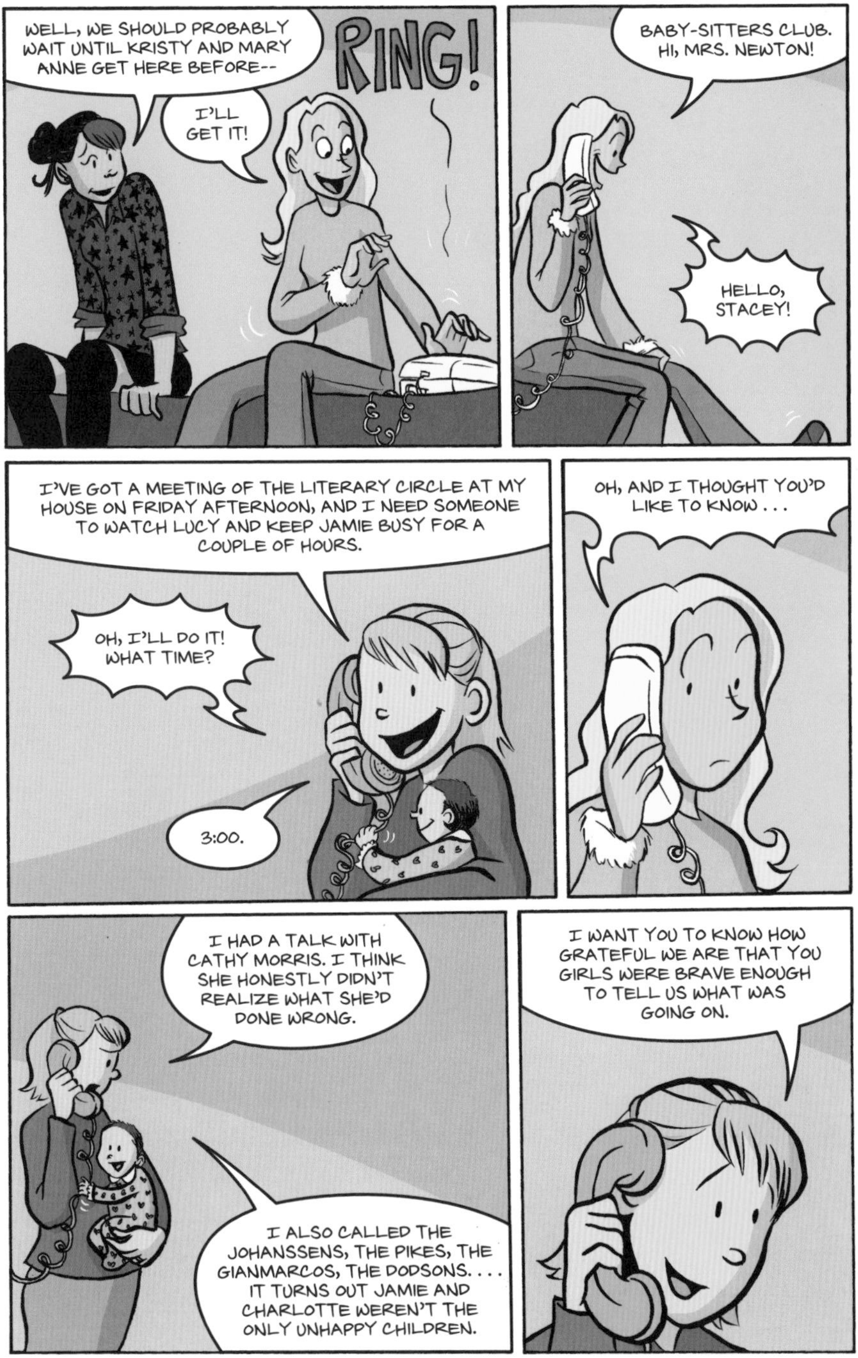
WELL, WE SHOULD PROBABLY WAIT UNTIL KRISTY AND MARY ANNE GET HERE BEFORE--
RING!
I'LL GET IT!
BABY-SITTERS CLUB. HI, MRS. NEWTON!
HELLO, STACEY!
I'VE GOT A MEETING OF THE LITERARY CIRCLE AT MY HOUSE ON FRIDAY AFTERNOON, AND I NEED SOMEONE TO WATCH LUCY AND KEEP JAMIE BUSY FOR A COUPLE OF HOURS.
OH, I'LL DO IT! WHAT TIME?
3:00.
OH, AND I THOUGHT YOU'D LIKE TO KNOW . . .
I HAD A TALK WITH CATHY MORRIS. I THINK SHE HONESTLY DIDN'T REALIZE WHAT SHE'D DONE WRONG.
I ALSO CALLED THE JOHANSSENS, THE PIKES, THE GIANMARCOS, THE DODSONS. . . . IT TURNS OUT JAMIE AND CHARLOTTE WEREN'T THE ONLY UNHAPPY CHILDREN.
I WANT YOU TO KNOW HOW GRATEFUL WE ARE THAT YOU GIRLS WERE BRAVE ENOUGH TO TELL US WHAT WAS GOING ON.

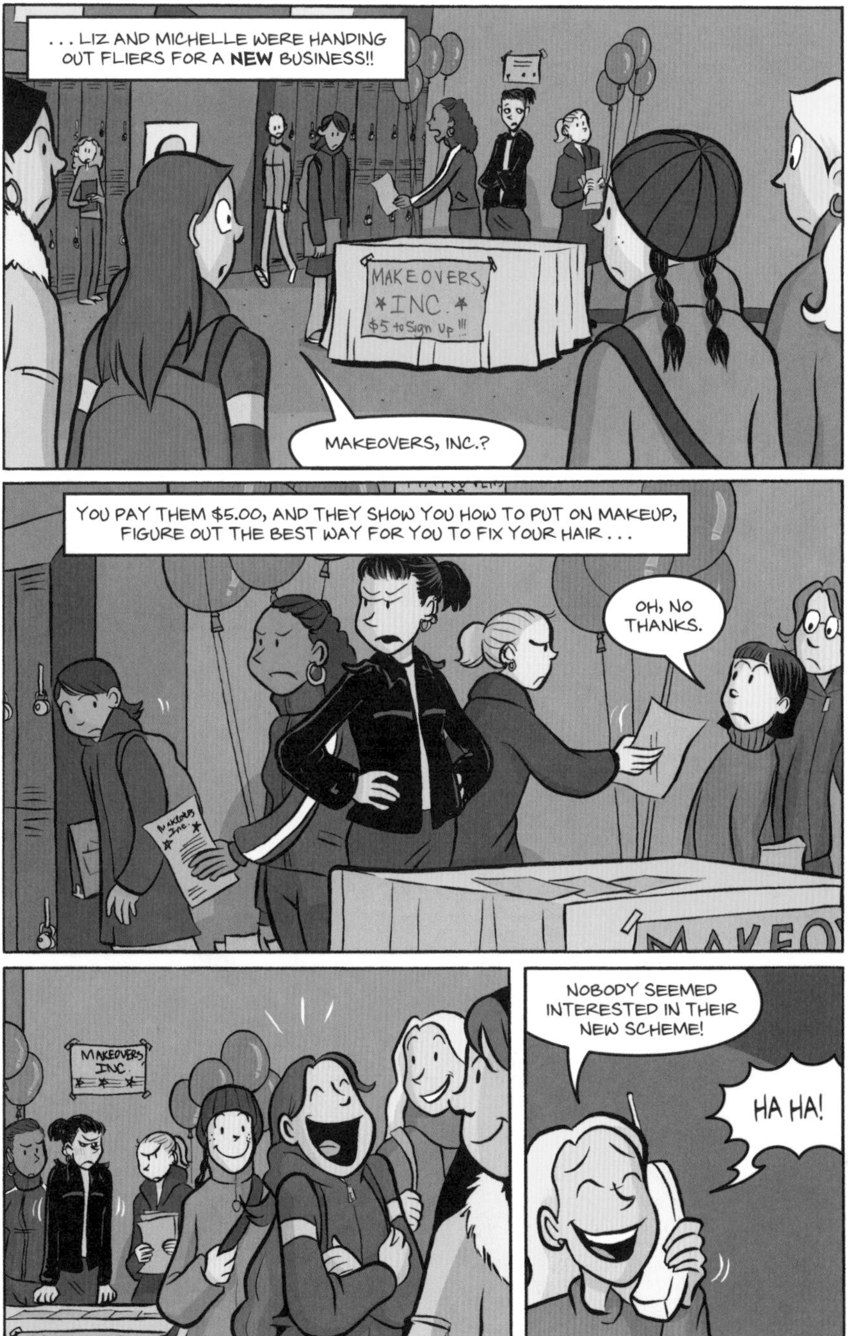

CHAPTER 15

. . . LIZ AND MICHELLE WERE HANDING OUT FLIERS FOR A **NEW** BUSINESS!!
MAKEOVERS, INC. $5 to Sign Up !!!
MAKEOVERS, INC.?
YOU PAY THEM $5.00, AND THEY SHOW YOU HOW TO PUT ON MAKEUP, FIGURE OUT THE BEST WAY FOR YOU TO FIX YOUR HAIR . . .
OH, NO THANKS.
MAKEOVERS INC.
NOBODY SEEMED INTERESTED IN THEIR NEW SCHEME!
HA HA!

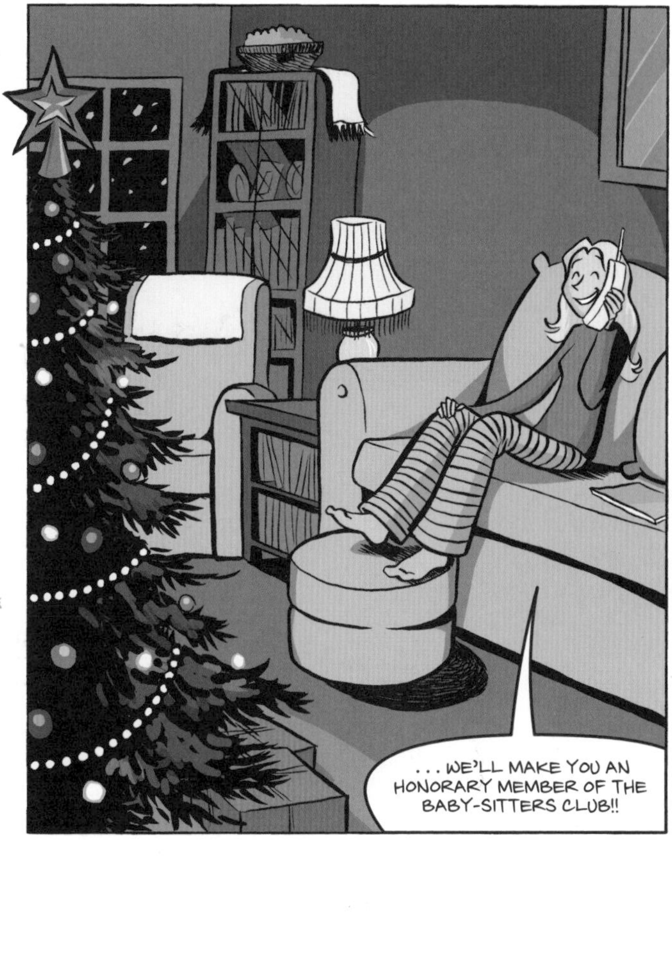
. . . WE'LL MAKE YOU AN HONORARY MEMBER OF THE BABY-SITTERS CLUB!!

This book is for my old pal, Claudia Werner
A. M. M.

Thanks to Marion Vitus, Adam Girardet, Duane Ballanger,
Lisa Jonte, Arthur Levine, and Braden Lamb. As always, a huge
thank-you to my family, my friends, and especially, Dave.
R. T.

Library of Congress Control Number: 2014945627

ISBN 978-0-545-81388-4 (hardcover)
ISBN 978-0-545-81389-1 (paperback)

10 9 8 7 6   16 17 18 19

Printed in Malaysia   108
First color edition printing, August 2015

Lettering by John Green
Edited by David Levithan, Janna Morishima, and Cassandra Pelham
Book design by Phil Falco
Creative Director: David Saylor